S0-BZN-296

ALSO BY
Katherine Applegate

KATHERINE APPLEGATE

illustrated by
MAX KOSTENKO

HARPER
An Imprint of HarperCollinsPublishers

Endling #3: The Only

Text copyright © 2021 by Katherine Applegate
Illustrations copyright © 2021 by Max Kostenko
All rights reserved. Printed in the United States of America.
No part of this book may be used or reproduced in any manner whatsoever without
written permission except in the case of brief quotations embodied in critical
articles and reviews. For information address HarperCollins Children's Books,
a division of HarperCollins Publishers, 195 Broadway, New York, NY 10007.
www.harpercollinschildrens.com

Library of Congress Control Number: 2020949342
ISBN 978-0-06-233561-6

Typography by Jenna Stempel-Lobell
22 23 24 25 26   PC/BRR   10 9 8 7 6 5 4 3 2 1
❖

First trade paperback edition, 2022

for Michael

Never doubt that a small group of thoughtful,
committed citizens can change the world;
indeed, it's the only thing that ever has.
—Margaret Mead

endling

noun ~ end•ling ~ \\`en(d)-ling\\

1. the last living individual in a species,
   or, occasionally, a subspecies.
2. the official public ceremony at which
   a species is declared extinct; a eumony.
3. (informal) someone undertaking a
   doomed or quixotic quest.

   —*Imperial Lexica Officio of Nedarra*, 3rd edition

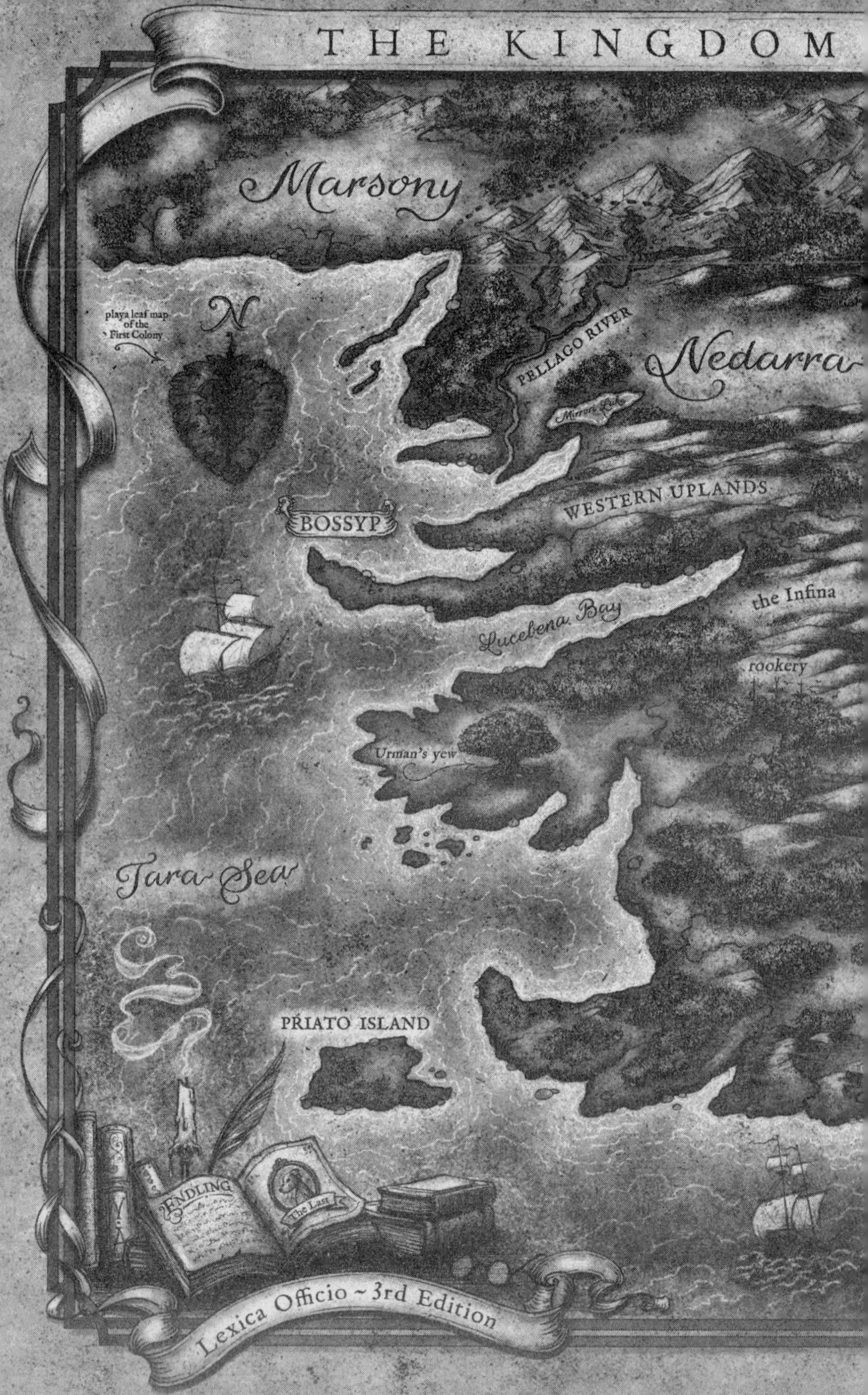

THE KINGDOM
Marsony
playa leaf map of the First Colony
N
PELLAGO RIVER
Nedarra
Mirror Lake
WESTERN UPLANDS
BOSSYP
the Infina
Lucebena Bay
rookery
Urman's yew
Tara Sea
PRIATO ISLAND
ENDLING
The Last
Lexica Officio ~ 3rd Edition

OF NEDARRA

Dreyland

SOVO RIDGE

ZEBARA   Landfail

PERRICCI MOUNTAINS   TAROK ISLAND
    Rebit's Sound   Dairneholm

    RHOMBOO ISLAND

SAGURIA

    Outpost   Chrisherna Sea

TELARNO RIVER

    ISLE OF URSINA
    (Cora di Schola)

    VELT

Therian Marshes   Grandia Sea

FOREST OF NULL

cave   mirabear hive

    Shark's Teeth rocks

    Pirates!

CONTENTS

PART THREE: HEART

PART ONE
EYES AND EARS

1
A Very Good Question Indeed

My name is Byx. I am a dairne.

What I am *not* is a great hunter.

So why did I volunteer to go hunting for eshwins with my friends Gambler and Sabito?

Good question. A very good question indeed.

"Do you smell them, Byx?" Gambler asked in his hoarse, rumbling voice. "Your nose is better than mine."

Gambler is a felivet, a huge catlike creature. His fur is black and shimmering as a river rock, save for the white lines striping his face. Sabito, a raptidon, is a great predator bird with a wingspan as wide as Gambler is long.

Gambler has speed, claws, and teeth. Sabito has speed, talons, and beak.

Me? I have a clumsy gait, silky white fur, and teeth that wouldn't frighten a kitten.

On the other hand, like dogs (to whom we bear more than a passing resemblance), dairnes do possess rather clever noses.

"I have their scent," I called from my perch on Havoc. My dappled silver horse was gingerly stepping over submerged stones in a shallow stream. "But I can't fix the direction with the wind so fitful."

When we reached the far bank, Havoc clambered up while I held on for dear life. The ground ahead was flat and fairly open, with widely spaced young trees, and we quickly caught up to Gambler as he raced along.

It's a wondrous thing, watching felivets on the hunt. They don't run so much as glide.

Sabito swooped down and leveled off just a few feet above us. He could hover for short periods, adjusting his wings a feather or two while using the lift of the sun's heat bouncing off the ground.

"They're just ahead," Sabito reported. "Do you see the meadow? Look beyond to the line of tall cypress trees."

Where my powers of scent had failed, his raptidon eyes had succeeded. How impressive are raptidon eyes? Sabito could read a book over my shoulder.

From a thousand feet away.

"Perhaps, friend Sabito," Gambler said, "you could get to their rear and be ready should they flee."

"I believe they intend to make a stand," Sabito replied.

"Well then," said Gambler, "dinner is served."

There was a time when felivets hunted my kind. That's no longer true. Still, it's hard to be a dairne near a hungry felivet and not feel a twinge of apprehension.

Felivet claws are like arrowheads. Their jaws can crush rocks. Gambler may be my dear and loyal friend, but he is also a ruthlessly efficient killer.

Which brought me back to my question. Why had I volunteered to go along on this hunt? Boredom? A feeling that I was a bit useless in the Army of Peace? A need to prove I wasn't afraid?

But of course I *was* afraid. A felivet, a raptidon, and a dairne against twelve hungry, frustrated eshwins? The odds were not in our favor.

Eshwins are strange creatures, a sort of cross between wild boars and bloated rats. They have vicious curved tusks and a habit of savaging easy targets: the young, the sick, the feeble. This particular pack of eshwins had attacked a family of cobblers, humans who were following the Army of Peace.

It's called the Army of Peace. It's not called the Army That Lets Eshwins Attack Others with Impunity. We were there to scare the eshwins off. If they could be scared off.

And if not? Well: Gambler.

We galloped into a wide meadow dotted with fading wildflowers, Havoc's hooves pounding the earth. The grass was up to his withers, high enough to conceal a crouching eshwin. But nothing—nothing—can hide from the eyes of a raptidon.

"Ambush ahead," Sabito warned. "They've split to your left and right and are waiting to close in behind you once you pass."

"We're ready," said Gambler.

Maybe *he* was. I wasn't.

I tightened my grip on Havoc's reins as he broke into a full-speed run. Wind ruffled my fur and filled my nostrils with a hundred scents, including the rank stink of eshwin and the sharp, metallic smell of my own fear.

"You have four behind you and eight ahead at the tree line," Sabito reported. "The four behind are closing in fast!"

"Byx," Gambler said, his voice eerily calm, "can you do something a bit crazy?"

"You mean like go on this hunt?" I asked, gasping for breath.

"Would you mind very much falling off your horse?"

"Would I . . . *what?*"

"I want them to think you're helpless."

"I *am* helpless!"

"That large tussock of gewgrass ahead would cushion your fall."

Gambler wanted to use me as bait. That was the only way I could be of use in the hunt.

We all have our strengths and our weaknesses and must contribute what we can. At least, that was what I told myself as Havoc closed the distance to the tussock.

I readied myself by slipping my left foot out of its stirrup. Closer. Hooves thundering.

Closer.

As I rolled off Havoc's right side I heard myself yelp. I hit the tussock hard enough to knock the air out of my lungs, but the grass and fungal mounds cushioned my fall and I was able to sit up.

Just in time to come face-to-tusks with a raging eshwin.

It charged, head down, and there was no way I could move in time.

The eshwin barreled toward me, grunting its guttural cry of triumph—*errrOOOT!*—and dribbling frothy saliva, anticipating the moment it would slice me open with its tusks.

"Noooo!" I yelled, pure terror in my voice, my limbs, my heart.

Which was when a black blur leapt from concealment, claws extended, mouth wide. Gambler hit the eshwin. Three seconds later the beast was ready to be skinned and cooked.

One down. Eleven left.

Three were still behind us, rushing at top speed, ripping through the meadow. But because of the tall grass, they were unable to see each other and were no doubt unaware that one of their number was already dead.

Sabito plunged from the sky like a falling star. He flared his wings, slowing, and struck one of the eshwins, sinking his talons into the creature's head.

Gambler, for his part, took care of the other two behind us. Three more eshwins were ready for the stewpot.

In the meantime, the eight eshwins hidden in the line of trees foolishly decided to come to the aid of their stricken pack members. They moved in a mass, grunting and squealing, a wall of rancid fur, gleaming tusks, and squinting red eyes.

Leading the charge was a creature so large she looked more like a horse than an eshwin. She was old, scarred from many battles. Battles she had probably won.

I saw Gambler's eyes go wide, which was not reassuring. "I will deal with their leader," he said, "but you, Byx, you had best flee."

"Flee?"

"I cannot take her and the rest all at once. *Flee!*"

Gambler moved to intercept the huge eshwin queen. Her fellow eshwins split left and right, aiming to encircle us while their leader fought Gambler.

Havoc had circled back to me. I grabbed his reins and hauled myself up into the saddle. The way back—retreat—was clear.

I'm no hunter, nor am I a soldier, and I am the furthest

thing from heroic. Every rational part of me agreed with Gambler: it was time to flee.

But Gambler was my friend.

More that that, he was family.

I drew my little sword and urged Havoc forward.

2
Creating Miracles

An hour and a half later, Sabito and I returned to the army camp. We were in central Nedarra, about a half-day march from the Telarno River.

We were bone-weary but pleased with our efforts, although Gambler had done most of the real work. After the last eshwin fell, Gambler decided to linger behind, content to "dine alone," as he put it.

"Byx! You're covered in blood!" my friend Tobble cried, running to meet us.

I dismounted from Havoc near the main campfire. "It's not my blood, Tobble."

"You're certain?" Tobble poked at me with his tiny paws, searching for injuries.

"I'm fine, Tobble. Better than fine. I hunted!"

"So I see," he muttered, glancing at the rough-hewn sled hitched to Havoc.

We'd laced together branches with knotted vines and piled three dead eshwins on top. The rest we'd left behind for our soldiers to retrieve. An army on the march always needs food.

"I should have been there." Tobble sent me an accusing look.

I hadn't told my faithful wobbyk companion about my plans. Where I went, Tobble inevitably followed, and I was doubtful enough of my own hunting abilities without having to worry about his well-being. Though he has the courage of an entire army, Tobble's just a fraction of my size. I feel as protective of him as he does of me.

We make an unusual pair, Tobble and I. While dairnes have doglike features, wobbyks look rather like well-fed foxes. They have large eyes, even larger ears, three tails, and a friendly, talkative nature. They're exceedingly courteous and seem, on the surface, utterly nonthreatening.

But those gentle exteriors hide warrior hearts. It's astonishing how insane wobbyks can be when pushed to extremes. I'd witnessed more than a few soldiers of the Murdano, our mortal enemy, fall victim to Tobble's fury.

"I'm sorry, Tobble," I said. "I should have invited you. To be honest, I feared I wasn't up to the task. And I didn't want to have to worry about you, too."

"I can take care of myself," he said, jutting out his chin.

I patted his back. "I am well aware of that."

Tobble grumbled under his breath. I made out the words "reckless" and "rash," and because Tobble is a wobbyk, and wobbyks are polite to a fault, I also heard "no offense" and "I'm sure you had your reasons."

I recognized one of the stewards who fed and watered the horses. "Dontee!" I called. "Run and tell the cooks they'll find many more eshwins just half a mile west. Send a wagon."

"Eshwins?" Dontee repeated with a gulp.

"Don't worry. They won't be hurting anyone anytime soon."

"So now you're the mighty hunter dairne?" Tobble teased. "Meaning no disrespect, my friend, but you really must wash yourself in the river. You stink of eshwin!"

"They are disgusting animals," I said. "And of no use except as food."

"Not 'of no use,'" Sabito chided in his harsh-sounding raptidon voice. I hadn't realized he was hovering just a few feet behind me, riding the breeze. "Eshwins dig up the roots of burrell trees, which helps the trees reproduce. And burrell trees, in turn, are home to many other species. No creature is useless, Byx. Each is a piece of a puzzle so vast that none can see it all."

I looked at the ground, chagrined.

"Forgive me," Sabito said, softening his tone. "I didn't mean to lecture. And I will concede that eshwins are not the most . . . lovable animals."

I managed a smile. But Sabito was right. Every species had something to contribute.

I, of all creatures, should know that.

Once upon a time, dairnes roamed Nedarra, our homeland, in great numbers. Now just a handful of us remained. For a while, in fact, I'd thought I was the last dairne in the world: an endling.

Dairnes have always been hunted for our downy fur. But that's not the only thing that's driven my kind to the edge of extinction. Far too many dairnes have been murdered because of our unique skill: the ability to tell when someone is lying.

It is the gift and the curse of my species.

Humans *want* our fur, but they *fear* our ability to detect a lie.

I've learned a little about humans recently. Their desires can be powerful, but their fears are far more so.

Although, in fairness, perhaps that's true of us all. These days, fear never seemed to leave my side, unshakable as a shadow.

"See the smaller one on the sled?" I asked, and I heard an unsettling mix of pride and shame in my voice. "That one was . . . mine."

"Once again," said Tobble, gazing at the limp and bloodied

carcasses, "I am grateful wobbyks are not meat eaters." He gave a little shrug. "'Remember we all have our place,'" he said. "'The bug, the bird, the human race.'"

"What was that?" asked Sabito.

"It's from a poem called 'A Young Wobbyk's Introduction to the World.'"

Sabito perched on a red-limbed mara tree. "I would rather like to hear it," he said. "Are raptidons mentioned?"

"All six great governing species are included." Tobble adjusted his carefully braided tails. "Also wobbyks. Naturally."

"Please, Tobble," I said. "I'd like to hear it, too."

"I'm not sure I recall it fully," he admitted. "But I shall try." Tobble cleared his throat. His voice was soft but clear.

Felivet, silent, stalks his prey.
Great cat shuns the light of day.

Terramant digs beneath the soil
In deep and dark and endless toil.

Natite swims the waters deep.
Seas and oceans are his keep.

Raptidon soars the cloudless skies
And scans the world with cunning eyes.

Dairne finds lies, a skill so rare
No other species can compare.

Human, never satisfied,
Too oft is moved by greed or pride.

Wobbyk, kind but fierce of heart,
Of all the world just one small part.

Remember we all have our place,
The bug, the bird, the human race,
As each day earth begins anew,
Creating miracles for you.

Tobble gave a little bow. I applauded and Sabito fluttered his wings. "I quite enjoyed that," said Sabito. "Even though we raptidons are not given to poetics, as a rule."

"'Creating miracles,'" I said, sighing. "I'd argue that miracles are in rather short supply these days."

"We'll get through this, Byx," Tobble said. "The Army of Peace will succeed. We have to."

I stared at the endless lines of dusty tents, stretching out before us like huge gravestones. "I wish I shared your optimism."

How weary I sounded to my own ears! How jaded! What had happened to the old Byx?

Not so long ago, I was just a silly pup. The runt of my litter. Self-involved, naive, impatient to see the world.

Well, I'd certainly gotten my wish. I'd seen far too much of the world. I'd seen enough pain and danger and death to last several lifetimes.

I was no longer Byx, the innocent daydreamer, curious and carefree. The pup who could gaze for hours at a swarm of rainbow-winged butterbats dancing on the wind.

The old Byx didn't gallop into battle to kill eshwins, yelling in triumph like a fool as they fell.

Perhaps Tobble was right that better times awaited us. Perhaps the old Byx was hiding somewhere deep in my heart.

Perhaps.

But for now I had to go wash the blood from my fur.

3
A Promise to Khara

That night I joined my comrades around a fire, one of hundreds that turned our camp into a twinkling reflection of the stars overhead. The eshwins made for a satisfying meal, and we were feeling drowsy and sated. (Tobble had dined on pan-fried crickets with maggot jelly.)

It was impossible to forget that war was brewing all around us, surrounded as we were by armed sentinels. Still, a welcome calm descended on me as I gazed at my dear friends. My old clan, slaughtered by troops of the Murdano, had been replaced by this new, multispecies family. Tobble. Gambler. Sabito. Renzo, the easygoing human who'd spent much of his young life as a skilled thief. Dog, his slobbering canine companion.

Maxyn, my fellow dairne, sat next to me. When we'd discovered his tiny, fragile colony of dairnes still alive, just knowing I wasn't an endling had seemed a kind of victory. But dairnes, it had turned out, were still endangered, walking the thin knife's edge over the precipice of extinction.

On my other side sat Kharassande Donati, now known as the Lady of Nedarra. Khara, my former captor, my rescuer, my friend, the person for whom I would give my life if needed.

When we'd first met, Khara had been pretending to be a boy while she served a gang of poachers. She'd captured me, saved my life, then saved it again and again. Now she led an army unlike any ever before assembled: the Army of Peace.

We'd gathered not to fight a war, but to stop one. Two powerful tyrants, the Murdano in my native Nedarra, and the Kazar Sg'drit in Dreyland to the north, were poised on the edge of conflict. Both of them wanted war, but their peoples simply wanted to live their lives in peace.

It was a strange and untried idea: an army whose sole purpose was preserving peace. More than a few of our soldiers had never lifted a sword. They were farmers, bakers, herbalists, clerks, blacksmiths, coopers, midwives, masons, and carpenters. Some were servants or apprentices. Others had been thralls, freed by us, for Khara refused to tolerate slavery in any form. Many of those marching with us were young and green. Others were so old that this would almost certainly be their last adventure.

Fortunately, we had experienced warriors as well, hard men

and women with sinewy muscles and appraising eyes. Some bore the visible scars of war. Even my friends and I had seen our share of danger in the months leading up to this moment.

As a crescent moon sailed the sky, we huddled together, telling stories and singing songs. Renzo, in fine voice, contributed an especially bouncy tune. It involved a lad in love with a fickle lass, and although I couldn't catch all the nuances—humans are impossibly confusing when it comes to affection—I noticed Khara rolling her eyes more than once, her soft brown skin flushed in the firelight.

After a while we fell quiet, and Khara motioned for me to join her for a private conversation.

"Would you like company?" Renzo inquired, standing.

Khara laughed. "Not in the least. This is between Byx and me."

"Your loss," Renzo said with a dramatic sigh, bowing with a flourish.

Khara's tent was identical to the one I shared with Tobble, although hers had a guard posted at the front flap, a burly young man clutching a long spear. He snapped a salute as we entered.

Khara lit a candle, then settled on her small cot, gazing at me thoughtfully. I sat on an overturned crate next to a makeshift table covered with maps.

"There's been an interesting development," she said.

"Interesting good? Or interesting bad?"

"I may have to ask you to undertake a mission."

I nodded. "Whatever you command, my lady."

"Byx, you're not one of my soldiers. You're a friend. I don't command you. I can only ask."

"Nevertheless, I will do as you . . . 'ask.'"

"I'm not yet certain, but if I need you, it could be dangerous. It involves the natites. They're feeling us out, trying to decide whether to support the Army of Peace"—Khara paused—"or to oppose us."

"Maybe I'm missing something. What can sea creatures do about a land war?"

"It's a good question, Byx, and the answer is that I don't know. Of the six governing species, the natites are the hardest to read. But if we can enlist their support, they could put an end to any plans by the Murdano to invade Dreyland by sea."

"I don't envy you having to figure this out," I said.

"The thing is, Byx, I won't be the one figuring it out." She gave me a knowing, conspiratorial smile. "*You* will be."

"Me?"

I think that's what I said. I may have managed nothing more than a yelp.

"The natites are asking us to send an ambassador. Someone to listen to their concerns."

"But I'm just . . . I'm just . . ."

"Byx. The days of 'I'm just a simple dairne' are over. If I can be the Lady of Nedarra, you can be Ambassador Byx."

"No I can't!" I cried.

Khara leaned forward, arms on her knees. "I can lead the army, Byx. But our goal is to stop a war, not engage in one. For that, we need diplomacy. And that means I need your help."

It was such a simple statement. If Khara needed me to do something, then I would do it or die trying.

Although I didn't have to be happy about it.

"Would I be alone?" I asked, aware of a cold ache in the pit of my stomach.

Khara shook her head, and her dark curls glistened in the candlelight. "Alone? No, of course not. For a start, no power I know of could separate you and Tobble. So clearly our excitable but ever-polite wobbyk will accompany you. I wish I could send Gambler with you, but, well, felivets and water . . ."

I smiled, recalling the sight of mighty Gambler tiptoeing nervously into a shallow subterranean lake.

"Maxyn isn't well enough to travel. And Sabito? If felivets don't like water, raptidons like it even less."

"Renzo?"

"Renzo," Khara repeated, and I could have sworn the idea of him leaving her side made her wistful. "Yes, I suppose he might prove of use." She nodded. "Yes, Renzo. Absolutely."

"When do we leave?"

"It's just a few hours to the Telarno, where we'll set up camp near a town on the river. The next morning we'll meet the natite ambassador. He'll take you, Tobble, and Renzo by watercraft to the natite queen's palace. There you'll listen to her thoughts and present her with the Subdur natite shield and crown we . . . borrowed."

We hadn't so much borrowed those items as stolen them. But in fairness, we'd been afraid for our lives at the time.

"I'll do my best," I said.

"I know you will," said Khara.

We both stood, but as I moved to leave, Khara took hold of my arm. "Byx," she said, "I have loyal generals and a devoted army. And I count Renzo, Tobble, Gambler, and Sabito as the truest of friends. But it's you, more than anyone, I'll be counting on in the days ahead."

"Me," I repeated. "Why me?"

"Because we've been through so much together. And because I know I can always count on you to tell me the truth." Khara glanced at the wrinkled pile of maps on her little table. "I've done my best to plan for what's ahead, Byx. But one thing I know: the battlefield laughs at plans."

I managed a small smile.

"As I see it, we face three important challenges as we try to stop this war. The first is to ensure that the natites are on our side. For that, I need you to be my eyes and ears. You'll talk to the natite queen, watching for signs of duplicity and listening for reasons to trust her."

"I can do that," I said, although I could hear the doubt in my own voice.

"The next challenge," Khara continued, "will be to recruit others to our cause. I'll need you to be the voice of the Army of Peace. To explain our mission and secure loyalty. You'll need to be convincing, if you sense they are wavering. Dairnes are trusted by other species, and we shall use that to our advantage."

"I can do that," I said again, and this time my uncertainty was obvious.

Khara put both hands on my shoulders and smiled. "How lucky I am to have you by my side, Byx," she whispered.

"You didn't say what the third challenge is."

"The first two problems are diplomatic, but the last . . ." Khara's hands dropped to her sides. "If—when—the Army of Peace comes face-to-face with the Murdano's army and the Kazar's forces, we'll either stop the war and prevail, or we'll die trying."

I gulped past the sharp rock that seemed to have lodged in my throat. "You can count on me, Khara. I promise to be your eyes and ears, as well as your voice."

"My eyes and ears, my voice, and my heart as well." Khara's eyes were glistening. "Now get some sleep. You are about to go on an adventure."

"A dangerous adventure," I murmured.

"Byx, my friend. Is there any other kind?"

4
On the March

Early the next morning we headed across the rolling plains of Nedarra, four abreast, five thousand strong, a column bristling with tall lances. The day was clear and cool, the sun bright. Now and then a helmet or breastplate would catch a beam of light and practically blind me with the glare.

Perhaps a tenth of us rode horses. The rest, mostly humans, marched on sore feet. We'd been on the road for many weeks, but our spirits were high.

Many of the horsemen and -women in the column wore either the blue of the Donatis or the orange of the Corplis. But Khara had asked a group of seamstresses to come up with a new livery in colors that would represent a united Nedarra, and she already wore the first of those tunics. It was pale blue, emblazoned with a vivid green representation of Urman's yew, the tree where a great interspecies peace pact had been made many years ago.

Still, it wasn't Khara's tunic that caused our soldiers to whisper and nudge each other. It was the sword at her side. The famous weapon, wreathed in theurgic spells, appeared plain, even shabby, until drawn in anger. When that happened, its power was breathtaking. One glance at that glowing blade, and it was clear why it was called the Light of Nedarra.

After an hour of riding, I urged Havoc into a trot and came level with Khara. Her chief general, Varis, politely moved his big steed aside to let me approach. General Varis, recently promoted, was a member of the Corpli family, long enemies of the Donatis but now allies with the Army of Peace.

On Khara's other side rode Bodick the Blue, a woman of middle age who had lost an ear and an eye in a long-ago battle, and three fingers on her left hand in another. She was called "the Blue" because she had covered a gruesome scar on her cheek with an indigo tattoo of a coiled serpent.

I'd grown quite fond of Bodick. She was not, perhaps, the type of person you'd invite to tea. But she was most definitely the sort of warrior you wanted nearby if battle came your way.

"How are you feeling, Byx?" Khara asked.

"A bit preoccupied, to be honest," I said.

"You needn't be. I have complete faith in you."

I decided to change the subject. "How much farther are we traveling today?"

"We'll be asking permission to make camp outside the

fortified village near the river. We should get there before noon."

"They can hardly say no to an army," said General Varis. It sounded like a threat, but then, everything the huge, red-haired human said seemed threatening. Once, when General Varis had politely asked Tobble for a drink from his water-skin, the little wobbyk had practically fainted.

"True, General," Khara agreed. "But we must honor whatever decision they make. This is the Army of Peace, and peace we will have."

"Unless, of course, we are attacked," General Varis countered, sounding vaguely hopeful.

Khara nodded. "Unless."

"Are you expecting an attack, General?" I asked.

"I can't lie in the presence of a dairne," he said, with a trace of what might have been a smile. "Some of our people would love a small battle."

Bodick patted her sword. "Just—you know—to break up the routine," she said.

"Let's hope they remain frustrated," Khara said. "But if we are attacked, you can be certain we'll defend ourselves with such righteous fury that no one will dare test us again."

Sometimes, even to my own seasoned ears, Khara sounded nearly as terrifying as her generals. Had she changed as much as I had? Or had she simply embraced her larger self, the leader she was meant to become?

And what had I become? Certainly not Byx the ambassador, despite Khara's confidence.

Gambler loped over, with Tobble astride his back. Riding Gambler had proven to be more comfortable for Tobble than sitting behind me on Havoc. And in spite of his complaining, Gambler seemed to enjoy the company.

"When do we stop to eat?" Tobble asked me. "My breakfast was much too light. Caterpillars never seem to satisfy me. Too much fuzz."

"I don't think we'll be stopping," I answered. "See that walled village beside the Telarno River in the distance? The plan is for us to camp there outside the walls."

"Never fear, Tobble," said Khara with a smile. "It's just a league and a half, at most."

"My apologies," Tobble said, "but my stomach is not as polite as my head. It won't stop grumbling."

I couldn't help laughing. Dairne stomachs whine when we're hungry. By comparison, grumbling has always seemed rather . . . obvious.

"Even after all that eshwin yesterday, I wouldn't object to a little snack," said Gambler, glancing over his shoulder at Tobble. "And as it happens, I have a perfectly tasty morsel riding on my back."

"On your back?" Tobble twisted around to look, then caught himself. "Oh, I see. But of course you're just teasing," he said, patting Gambler's flank.

"Am I?" Gambler asked, a glint in his pale blue eyes.

"Gambler," Khara said, "we do not eat our comrades."

"Agreed," said Gambler. "Unless they annoy us."

I winked at Gambler. He smiled back, although a felivet smile is hard to distinguish from a felivet snarl, and both are unnerving. "I'd be careful, Tobble," I warned. "Gambler does look a bit hungry."

"Not funny, Byx," said Tobble. "Not funny at all. Stop being silly."

"You know, Tobble, I might be described as silly, but I'm pretty sure Gambler has *never* been called that."

"Silly," Gambler repeated with a grimace. "I could eat you just for that."

Behind us, a sergeant started a chant to keep his soldiers moving at the same speed, his gruff baritone setting the pace.

Your left. Your left. Your left, right, left.
The spears on our backs are sharp and long,
The Army of Peace is mighty and strong.
Heed well the warning in this, our song:
We'll have your heads if you do us wrong.

I'd come to know these chants well, and sometimes even joined in. The soldiers called them "cadences." The rhymes were often humorous, and just as often belligerent.

I found myself humming along to the cadence call, but I

couldn't really keep time because my horse didn't care what the sergeant yelled. Havoc chose his own pace, thank you very much. One of four horses gifted to us by Khara's family, he was small enough for a dairne my size to manage. Most of the time, anyway.

A few minutes later, we neared a small pond, its surface still as ice. A large tree anchored one end, and a nest of chittering blue squirrels sat suspended over the water on a thick black branch.

It reminded me instantly of my favorite place when I was small, the sandy shore of a deep water hole called Phantom Mere, far from any village or road. We like swimming, we dairnes, another trait we share with many dogs. This particular lake was overhung by criller trees, which generate thick, dangling vines covered with glossy, pale yellow leaves. My siblings and friends would climb the trees, seize the vines, and swing out over the water.

Some of the more adventurous ones would spread their glissaires, the fine extensions of our coats that allow us to glide like flying squirrels. Those attempts invariably led to sudden plunges, huge spouts of water, and gales of laughter.

It had always looked like fun, but I never tried it myself. The lake was cold and dark, and its name didn't help matters. I was afraid.

"Come on, Byx! Don't be such a pup!" my older siblings used to tease me.

"I will . . . just not today," I'd always answered, though I'd never found the nerve to join in.

It might seem strange that I'd count a time of embarrassment and timidity as a precious memory. But every single recollection of those days was sacred to me now. They were all I had left of those I loved, and those who loved me in return. Sometimes, late at night, those memories seemed more real to me than my current strange existence.

Still, the thought of my younger self, trembling at the edge of that water hole, brought a rueful smile to my face. I'd been afraid of a body of water that held nothing more alarming than a few glimmering fish.

Had you told me then that a day would come when I'd spread my glissaires, leap from a tall building, and glide into the path of the Murdano's evil sorceress, I'd have rolled my eyes. Had you told me I'd stand boldly before the Murdano himself, or lead a dread Knight of the Fire into a trap, or find a way to attack a fleet of Marsonian ships, I'd have laughed out loud.

I turned in my saddle to catch one more glimpse of the little pond. Behind me, dust hovered over the army as it marched along. One of the soldiers tossed a stone into the placid water. The rock vanished into the darkness with barely a ripple.

5
The Night Before

Just before noon we reached the walled village, which we learned from a passing farmer was called Callumweir. It looked less and less impressive the closer we got. The walls weren't much higher than a tall human. Gambler could have cleared them in a single bound.

Khara went to parley with their mayor, a tall, flaxen-haired man named Tarang the Pale, and took me along as her truth teller. We returned after half an hour with permission to camp our troops outside his town. When the townsfolk learned of our mission, twenty-three of them volunteered to join the Army of Peace, including Tarang himself, who resigned as mayor and arrived in camp hefting a double-edged ax.

We pitched our tents, laid out bedrolls, dug latrines, and tended to the horses, a tedious routine that had become second nature. Khara had sent an advance party into the forest to cut logs for a rough palisade, a circular barrier of pointed stakes set into the ground to block intruders. Erecting it was a huge job and one that lasted well beyond sunset, but Khara insisted that every camp be strong enough to defend. If we were attacked, we wouldn't easily be overrun. And when we moved on, the palisade would remain behind for the use of the villagers, if they wished it.

That evening I stopped by Maxyn's tent, which he shared with Renzo and Dog. He was alone, settled on a blanket near a flickering candle stub. A wooden crutch lay on the floor. Maxyn had been badly injured when he was taken captive by some of the Murdano's soldiers, and he was still recovering from his wounds.

We touched noses. "How are you feeling, Maxyn?"

"Better every day, Byx."

I gazed down at him. His eyes were darker than mine, his shoulders wider. He had fur the color of straw and long, silky ears. We were different in many ways, as you'd expect from individuals in a species.

Still, Maxyn was my mirror. When I looked at him, I saw myself. So few dairnes were left in the world that I felt a little shock of familiarity each time we crossed paths.

"You're staring again, Byx."

"Oh . . . sorry," I said, flustered. "It's just that when I see you, I sort of see me."

"And that's a bad thing?"

"No. No, of course not! But it makes me remember how alone we are. Dairnes, I mean."

"When I see you, I feel relieved," Maxyn said. "And happy."

I smiled. "How's the leg?" I pointed to a dusty splint on his right foot.

"Well, I won't be racing into battle anytime soon, but it's improving." Maxyn shifted position, grimacing. "How are you feeling about tomorrow? I wish I could go with you."

During dinner, Khara had shared the details of my mission with her closest advisers. Like me, Tobble and Renzo were determined to do their best. Also like me, they were extremely nervous about visiting the realm of the natites. There was nothing normal about air-breathing species spending time far beneath the sea.

"Natites give me the shivers," said Maxyn. "Strangest creatures I've ever seen. Except maybe for terramants."

Terramants are giant insect-like creatures with triangular heads and gnashing jaws. Natites come in many shapes and sizes, but all are water-breathers with multiple gills. Their heads are shaped like the bow of a ship, and they have tentacles, arms and legs, webbing between their fingers, and long feet ending in flexible fins.

"I know what you mean," I said, trying not to think about the trip ahead of me, where there would be no shortage of natites. "Although I think terramants are more terrifying. Those six spiny legs and the bulbous eyes! They remind me of the assassin spiders we used to find under rocks when I was little. Only a thousand times bigger." I sighed. "At least natites look vaguely familiar. Sort of part human, part fish."

Maxyn nodded. "You'll leave first thing in the morning?"

"The natite ambassador is meeting Renzo, Tobble, and me at a bend in the river not far from here. Khara will introduce us, and then . . . well, who knows?"

"You'll be fine," Maxyn said with a wink, and his confidence made me feel a bit better.

We talked for a while longer, and then I headed to the tent Tobble and I shared. Technically, it was Gambler's tent as well, but he preferred to stay outside, stalking the periphery of the camp. Felivets are nocturnal by nature, and, though Gambler tried to adapt to our daylight marches, it was difficult for him to suppress his instinct to roam at night.

I slept uneasily and awoke before dawn, surprised not to hear Tobble's familiar seesaw snoring. He was wide awake, staring at the tent ceiling, paws clutching his worn green blanket.

"Tobble?" I said. "Are you all right?"

He sat up, ears quivering, a forced smile on his face. "Of course I'm all right. I'm right as rain, whatever that means. Why wouldn't I be all right?"

"Because you're about to travel underwater to a palace full of fish people?"

Tobble gave a little laugh. "I'm just glad we're going together, Byx."

"I wouldn't have it any other way."

When Tobble and I emerged from our tent, laden down with our heavy packs, Khara, Renzo, and Dog were already waiting. The cooks had prepared a large iron pot simmering with tea, and we each ladled some into mugs.

"I want to go over this again so you're all clear," Khara said. "The natites are unknown to us, for the most part. We have no idea what they want. But if we're to stop this war between Nedarra and Dreyland, they could be extremely helpful."

"Do you really think the natites could stop a Nedarran naval movement?" Tobble asked.

"No ship moves upon the deep without the permission of the natites," said Khara. "Which is why"—she looked straight at Renzo—"you must be on your best behavior."

Renzo patted Dog's head. "So no stealing unless I think they won't notice it?"

"The first three words of what you just said? Stop there."

"Fine." Renzo made an exasperated face. "Why are you sending me if I can't even pick up a few baubles?"

"Because, despite all appearances, and despite most of

what you say, Renzo, you are not entirely witless, and I think Byx may actually profit from your advice."

"Also, you're the only one big enough to carry that shield," said Gambler as he sauntered over to join us.

Khara put a finger to her lips. "Shhh, don't tell Renzo he's just a beast of burden."

"I would like to strenuously object, just one more time, to the idea that we are going to give away the Subdur crown and shield to another natite queen," said Renzo. "I braved molten lava to reach those objects. Without my breathtaking agility and my awe-inspiring bravery, we wouldn't have them." He grinned. "Also, they're worth a fortune, and then some."

The crown and shield were artifacts claimed by the Subdur natites, a small and extremely odd renegade natite group that lived in a vast underground lake. One of the objects, which Tobble had dubbed a "Far-Near," was a miraculous tube that made distant objects appear close. Unfortunately, we'd had to part with it, but we still possessed a dramatic, jewel-encrusted crown and a large shield.

"I've long suspected that the crown, the shield, and the Far-Near were stolen by the Subdur clan from other natites," said Khara. "Their queen, Lar Camissa, certainly spoke evasively when she discussed them with us." She shrugged. "In any case, offering these gifts to the dominant natite ruler helps prove our sincerity and commitment. It's all part of diplomacy, Renzo. Sorry."

Renzo had the shield strapped to his back, camouflaged by burlap wrapping. He carried a small leather bag, which he handed to me.

"I've got the shield," he said with a sigh. "But I'm not sure I trust myself with the crown."

Khara shook her head. "Well, you know yourself best."

I removed the crown and slid it into my pouch. Like marsupials, dairnes have pouches on our stomachs. The crown was uncomfortable—a bit pointy—but I knew it would be easier than carrying an extra bag along with my usual pack and my sword. They don't mention it in the epic stories of long-ago heroes, but even small swords like mine are surprisingly heavy.

"So. The decision is yours to make, Byx," said Khara. "Do you trust these natites or not? Do you believe they can and will help the Army of Peace? We don't have weeks and weeks to play games. We need to know the natite mind. This is the first diplomatic step in our effort to stop the war. And it may prove to be the most important."

"I—I'll try," I said. My quavering voice betrayed me, and my stomach was churning like a rough sea. I truly didn't need Khara to remind me that I was carrying a giant load of responsibility.

I might help stop a war and save thousands of lives.

Or not.

"Gambler," said Renzo, "since this trip will be brief and

we need to travel light, I'm entrusting Dog to your care in my absence."

Dog attempted to give the felivet a sloppy kiss, but he was met with a paw nearly as big as Dog's head.

"You two play nice," said Renzo, and Gambler snarled.

"So. Are we ready, my friends?" I asked, trying to sound resolute.

"Always," Renzo replied, but Tobble shook his head.

"Breakfast first. If I'm going to die, I plan to do it on a full stomach."

6
Ambassador Byx

Just downstream from the village, the Telarno River made a lazy bend, forming a muddy brown pool shaded by willows. It was a short distance from camp, so Khara, Renzo, Tobble, and I approached on foot. Bodick and three soldiers followed behind us at a respectable distance. Khara wanted to send a clear message that the Army of Peace was just that: peaceful.

The natite was awaiting our arrival, or so Khara assured me. Still, I saw nothing.

"Ambassador! Ambassador Delgaroth!" she called.

The water parted with barely a ripple as he rose to the surface. Delgaroth was the deep blue of the sky just before night, with dazzling green markings on his flanks and face. His eyes were large for a natite, with dark blue irises surrounded by soft turquoise. When he blinked, it was with one or both of his two sets of eyelids. The first set was opaque, the second translucent. I'd been told that the clear eyelids allowed natites to see beneath the water.

"Good morning to you, Ambassador," said Khara with a nod.

"And to you, Lady Kharassande of the Donatis," Delgaroth said.

I was surprised by how easy he was to understand. Natites struggle to enunciate clearly when they're breathing air. He also spoke quite loudly, almost shouting, perhaps because he normally spoke underwater.

"I present my very good friends and companions, Renzo and Tobble, and my ambassador, Byx of the dairnes," said Khara.

I gulped, hearing the words "my ambassador" spoken aloud. I had to remind myself that Khara was talking about *me*.

Delgaroth barely glanced at Renzo and Tobble. Instead he focused his intense gaze on me.

"You are the dairne."

"As you see," I said, somewhat embarrassed. I felt as if I should bow, which would have been ridiculous.

Delgaroth pursed his dark red lips, taking us all in. "Our journey will take most of two days."

"Is there a boat?" Renzo asked, though there was no craft in sight.

"A boat of a different sort than perhaps you are used to."

Delgaroth pointed with one of his six tentacles. "It lies at the bottom of the river."

Renzo and I exchanged an uncomfortable look.

"Yes," Renzo whispered, "he said 'at the bottom.'"

I'd been afraid of this. We'd already had the bizarre experience of traveling underwater once before, courtesy of natite theurgy. Suspended in giant bubbles, we'd survived, but it had been surreal and disturbing, to say the least.

Delgaroth climbed out of the water and sat on the riverbank. "Can each of you swim?" he asked.

We could, though no one was happy about the idea of demonstrating. Renzo said, "I'm carrying this, um . . . heavy object. To be honest, I think it would be hard for me to swim with it."

"Do you care to name the object?" Delgaroth inquired politely.

I spoke up before Renzo could. "Perhaps later, when we meet your queen, we will have time for the telling of stories."

Delgaroth let my response pass, although he sent a puzzled look my way. "If you are ready, I invite you to board my humble craft. You have only to wade into the river. You will be quite safe, I assure you, encased in thousands of tiny bubbles. But be careful not to let the river's current knock you over. You land creatures are forever falling over."

"As the leader of this expedition, Byx," Renzo said, taking a step back, "you clearly should go first."

"Nonsense," I argued, "I should go last."

"*I'm* certainly not going first," Tobble said. He was a capable swimmer, but that didn't seem to be moving him.

In the end, we agreed to go at the same time. The riverbank was about a foot higher than the water itself, which meant the first step would be a jump, an uncertain plunge into the depths. We automatically took deep breaths and then, with Renzo counting down on his fingers—one, two, three—we leapt into the unknown.

And splashed into ankle-deep water.

I am no judge of natite faces, but I am quite sure Delgaroth was trying his best not to laugh at us.

Khara, on the other hand, was doubled over laughing.

Thus began my ambassadorship.

How do I explain the odd sensation of walking into a river, water surrounding you on all sides, while remaining completely dry? It was theurgy, of course, and it was never a good idea to rely too much on magic, but Delgaroth's spells were powerful. Even up to my neck in the icy brown water, I was dry.

"It grows deeper quickly," Delgaroth warned as he jumped back into the river. "I will guide you."

I paused and watched as Renzo took a step—the water was only up to his waist—then another tentative step. Another few inches and he toppled forward, arms flailing. "Aah!" he cried as he disappeared under the rushing river.

He was up in a flash, standing in chest-high water, which

was to say well above my head and far above Tobble, who was still near the bank.

"Hey, it's working!" Renzo said. "And it tickles!"

"Here goes," I said. I held my breath and submerged. To my delight and relief, the tiny theurgic bubbles extended up and over my head. I took a cautious breath. The bubbles rushed into my nose, popping and fizzing.

Air!

If walking underwater is hard, breathing is harder. Every instinct screams *don't!* And yet there I was, breathing underwater in tight little gasps that prickled my throat and made me want to laugh.

Although I'd visited the underwater realm before, this was quite different. Instead of an occasional wave, we faced a constant current. As Delgaroth had predicted, I had a difficult time keeping my feet under me.

"Help!" I heard a garbled Tobble through the shallow water. "I'm sorry, I don't mean to be a problem, but *help!*"

Tobble's tiny legs kicked frantically as he rushed past me, enclosed in his own bubble. I snatched at his foot but missed. Renzo, on the other side, was unable to do anything but flail.

Away went Tobble, a wobbyk in a bubble.

And not a happy wobbyk.

I was about to pop to the surface and swim after him, but I caught a flash of something shooting past at amazing speed. Delgaroth, in his natural element. The natite ambassador grabbed Tobble easily. He reached into a silver pack slung over his shoulder and handed Tobble a small brick.

"Hold on to this, friend wobbyk," Delgaroth said. "It's kurz. A heavy metal found beneath the sea."

With the kurz in his hands, Tobble was weighed down just enough. I could keep his feet on the riverbed by gripping his shoulder.

"Well, that was exciting," he said, voice shaky.

"We'll be all right," I said.

"I'd be more convinced if I couldn't feel your hand trembling."

"I have more kurz," said Delgaroth, glancing at Renzo and me, "if it's needed."

We both shook our heads. With the shield and crown as ballast, we were having an easier time than Tobble.

"Follow me, and if you have any further difficulty, you need only scream," Delgaroth called.

"Oh, we'll scream, all right," said Renzo. His voice, like mine and Tobble's, was muffled. Strangely, Delgaroth's voice had actually grown clearer. Something in the nature of natite voices made them sound almost musical underwater.

A big catfish swam by, eyeing me disapprovingly. I felt the constant push of the water, but by leaning into it I was able to keep my footing. The riverbed, something I'd rarely glimpsed from the surface, was a mix of colorful, swirling sand and sparkling rocks. Here and there I saw tangled strings of riverweed and occasional patches of what looked like tall, blue-striped grass.

At last, near what must have been the midpoint of the river, we came to something that was not sand or rock, weed or fish. It was a craft, floating above the riverbed at about twice my height. Though not nearly as grand as an ocean-going ship, it was perhaps ten times as long as I was tall. And it lacked one vital element of a sailing ship: it had no sail. Pointed at both back and front, it glistened in a muted rainbow that changed colors with each new shaft of light.

"It is called a barcabrena," Delgaroth explained.

"What's it made of?" I asked, hoping for reassurance.

"Horn," Delgaroth said. "Two horns, in fact. From narvaliks, a type of fish."

"Horns? On a fish?"

Delgaroth may have smiled. "There are many more mysteries in the deep places than you can imagine, Ambassador Byx."

And there it was, coming from the mouth of a natite: Ambassador Byx.

It was the first time I'd ever had a title, and it seemed much too grand for the likes of me. But that was what I was: Khara's ambassador. A dairne speaking to natites on behalf of a human.

Life will surprise you sometimes.

Sometimes I wish it would stop doing that.

7
Beneath the River

As I inspected the outside of the barcabrena, I saw that it was indeed made of horn. Two horns, in fact, as the natite had said, connected at their bases and hollowed out to make a watertight compartment within. I shuddered to think just how huge a narvalik had to be in order to maneuver such an appendage. Even more fantastic, the barcabrena was harnessed to dozens of identical fish: huge orange-spotted bass, as big as me, all in mesh harnesses made of woven seaweed.

Unlike a typical boat, it had neither masts nor decks. Instead there were two round hatches, one on the top and one on the bottom. Delgaroth opened the bottom hatch and motioned to Renzo. I watched as Renzo crouched beneath the submerged craft, then stood, his top half disappearing into the interior. From there he pulled up his legs and disappeared from view.

"It's dry inside!" he called.

I don't know whether it was simply a law of nature or natite theurgy, but sure enough, water did not seem to be rushing in through the hole.

"Shall we?" I asked Tobble, who still gripped his weighty brick.

"Lift me up. Please."

I eased Tobble into the hatch, then climbed up after him. The interior of the barcabrena was indeed dry, and far more ornate than I would have imagined. Oblong green jewels and round azure crystals dotted the walls and ceiling at regular intervals.

I glanced at Renzo.

"What?" he demanded, fingers pressed to his chest. "I was absolutely not thinking what you're thinking I was thinking."

"You realize I'm a dairne, right?"

"Maybe I *thought* about it. Just thought. Then I realized if I got caught, our friend Delgaroth might drown me."

As if on cue, Delgaroth rose through the hatch with far more grace than we had managed. He shot upward, cleared the hole, and closed the hatch.

"Here you will be perfectly safe and dry." He said "dry" as if the word had a sour taste. "From time to time I will summon dolphins. They'll blow in fresh air so that you don't become sleepy."

"Or dead," Renzo muttered.

The room we were in wasn't large, but it occupied half of the craft, with a small section at the rear with bunks for sleeping, and a larger area at the front closed off by bulkheads. With chairs and a table in the center, it felt like a cozy tavern.

"Are you all comfortable now?" Delgaroth asked politely.

Renzo nodded. "As comfortable as I ever am, when I'm in an underwater coffin."

"There are drinks in those bottles," Delgaroth said, waving a webbed hand at the table. "I believe they will suit you. If you are too warm or too cold, simply say it aloud. If you call out, I'll hear you and summon such creatures as are appropriate. Lavacore eels can warm the craft, and of course the water itself will cool things. I will be in the forward compartment or swimming alongside, as I find air difficult over longer periods. It's very . . . inhospitable."

Delgaroth excused himself, exiting to the forward compartment through a silver door. I heard a rush of gurgling water as he sighed with relief.

The craft moved with a jerk as the harnessed fish began to move. Soon the ride became fairly smooth, interrupted with a little side-to-side rocking. Tobble, who came from a long line of mariners, walked around easily on what he called his "sea legs." Renzo, on the other hand, staggered about like a drunk, bashing his head into low portions of the ceiling. For my part, I leaned against the table for stability, trying to adjust to the erratic movement.

Delgaroth had shown us a hatch in the top of the craft from which, he claimed, we could safely emerge to watch our trip unfold. With some reluctance, I decided to give it a try. As I climbed on a stool and opened the hatch, a single large blister of air rose, remarkably, to encase my head. Poking out from the top of the barcabrena, I could truly feel our speed as the yoked bass churned the water into sparkling bubbles. It was exhilarating. My pulse quickened, and I couldn't stop myself from grinning. I was seeing a world that had always been there, one that I'd never thought I could know. One the old Byx would never have dared visit.

The bed of the river had its own fascinating geography. Blue and yellow sand whirled in intricate patterns, delicate as lace. Spiky black rock formations appeared suddenly, sending the current into furious foaming. The yoked fish skirted these obstacles effortlessly, though at times they cut it so close I feared they'd rake our craft over the rocks and drown us all.

As the river deepened and widened, the banks vanished from sight. We kept to the midpoint between the surface and the riverbed, shooting along faster than the swiftest steed. After a while I felt Tobble tugging at my leg. Reluctantly, I dropped back down into the craft's dry interior. Magically, my protective bubble evaporated.

"You should look, Tobble. You too, Renzo. It's amazing!"

"I'm sure it is," Tobble said. "But another amazing thing is my hunger."

"I could use a bite myself," Renzo agreed.

Instantly a servant arrived through the front compartment to serve us. For the first time, we realized that Delgaroth was not the only natite aboard. The servant was compact and pale yellow, with four spiraling tentacles, two sprouting from each shoulder.

"Will you try some of this?" he asked, presenting us with a plate of slivered fish and tiny crabs cooked in a fragrant sauce, along with bowls of what appeared to be a seaweed stew.

We sat at the table, and Tobble dipped a golden spoon into the stew. He took a taste and his eyes went wide. "It's delicious! What's it called?"

"Raakal," said the servant. "Does it please you?"

Tobble was too busy gulping down more, so I took a taste. "It does!" I exclaimed.

When I began to raise a bottle to my lips, the servant gently intervened, offering a strange, thin tube. "Natite ale is always consumed through one of these."

Renzo nodded approvingly. "Very clever. Natites can keep the liquid in the bottle distinct from the water this way."

"They are called drink reeds," the servant explained.

"I take it you have no fire you can use to cook?" I asked.

"No fire, but heat, yes. You will see as we near Jaureggia."

"I'm sorry," I said, frowning. "What was that last word?"

"Jaureggia. It is the great city and palace of Pavionne, our queen."

The servant left and I leaned back in my chair, full but uneasy. "Queen Pavionne," I repeated. I looked at my friends. "Let's hope she makes her intentions crystal clear. Just because I'm a dairne doesn't mean I'll be able to read her true desires."

"No one but the sea knows what natites want," Renzo said darkly. It was an oft-repeated saying.

"Perhaps," I mused, "no one ever asks them."

8
Sunrise and Sartel

I slept surprisingly well, given that we were moving underwater at the speed of a falcon in flight. The bunks in the back compartment were sized for humans and luxuriously large for me. Tobble actually found his bunk too spacious for comfort. In the main cabin he discovered a wooden crate, into which he stuffed a blanket. He curled up, as contented as a cat. A loudly snoring cat.

After hours of sleep I was awakened by a change in the soothing rocking motion. Too alert to fall back to sleep, I climbed up to the viewer hatch for a look. The water was the color of wine, dark and velvety, sliced with slanted beams of silver moonlight.

To my surprise, Delgaroth was in the water. He'd left the craft and was holding on to a hook attached to the side of the barcabrena.

He saw my inquisitive look and nodded. "You felt it?"

"I felt something," I said. My voice reverberated within the bubble, and I doubted he'd be able to hear me, separated as we were by swift-flowing water. But natite ears, like their voices, work best beneath the water.

"We're leaving the river and entering the ocean. Thus far we've been drawn by freshwater fish, but they'll soon fall away and return to their pools and inlets."

"How will we move after that?" I asked.

"If you are patient you will see, Ambassador."

Again, there was that daunting label: Ambassador. Each time I heard it, my chest tightened and I felt the queasy sense of being an imposter. I'm Byx, a dairne and nothing more, I wanted to protest. I'm playacting. A mere child pretending to be an adult.

I shook off the feeling as best I could, and, too curious to return to my bunk, I decided to continue my watch.

I soon realized it was well worth the wait.

I've seen many sunrises in my young life. But watching the sun blossom when you're underwater is an entirely different experience. That first spot of light melting on the river's surface. Long shafts of sun piercing the water like swords of pure gold. Shimmering bubbles of color, drifting down like discarded jewels.

I couldn't pull my gaze away, as grateful tears filled my eyes.

I might fail Khara. I might disappoint myself and my loyal friends. So much could go wrong, so quickly, on this mission of mine.

But I promised myself I would cherish the gift of that sunrise no matter what happened.

How the earth can surprise us if we let it!

We began to slow, as the yoked fish slipped their harnesses one by one, each turning sharply and swimming past my head. Finally we came to a stop, lolling sluggishly in the current. I heard Renzo rouse below. "Where are we?" he called.

"I'm not sure. The fish have left us, but Delgaroth says it's natural."

"Is there room for me up there?"

"Of course."

In truth, it was a tight fit, but the viewing bubble expanded enough to accommodate Renzo.

"Wow," he said. "That is . . . gorgeous."

It was a bit surprising to hear the word "gorgeous" come from Renzo's mouth, but he was indeed right. "Look!" he cried, pointing with his chin.

At first I didn't see it, not because it was too small, but because it was too big.

It was a creature.

A whale.

Seconds before it seemed ready to crash into our boat, the whale turned its enormous head upward. It flowed past, a gleaming gray wall gathering speed, impossibly long, huge beyond measure, bigger than any creature I could even imagine.

It shot upward, exploding through the early sun's hues and reflecting them all. Erupting from the water, it soared over the craft, turning day into night as the water above us darkened in its shadow.

"By all the ancients and their pet cats!" Renzo exclaimed. "It must weigh more than ten houses."

My heart stopped beating. I could not draw breath.

The beauty was impossible. The power unimaginable.

The whale plunged back down into the water. The impact was like a distant explosion. Our craft tilted and I heard Tobble spill from his crate, startled from his slumber.

"Help! We're sinking!" he cried.

"Come join us in the bubble," I called to him. "We're fine."

Tobble clambered up, perching on Renzo's shoulders like a child watching a parade.

"Oh, I see," Tobble said, yawning. "It's a sartel whale. They're common enough in these waters."

"Common?" Renzo and I said at the same time.

Tobble nodded. "Sartels are the third-largest whale, I believe."

"The third?" Renzo repeated. "Just how big are number two and number one?"

"Well, I've only seen them from the surface, but I'd say

a mature coralskimmer whale is twice as large. Then, of course, there's the spotted Renner's whale, which is so vast it could eat that sartel whale, this craft, and two or three good-sized sailing vessels."

Renzo and I stared at him with a mixture of amazement and fear. Neither of us liked the idea of a living thing so big it might see "our" whale as a snack.

"Don't worry." Tobble waved a paw. "Spotties are very slow. And they only eat seaweed and krill."

"I wasn't worried," Renzo said.

"Oh?" Tobble sent me a sly look. "Is that true, Byx?"

I laughed. "I refuse to answer, as it might embarrass Renzo."

I noticed Delgaroth floating near the whale's head. When the sartel grabbed the seaweed harnesses in its massive jaw, Delgaroth swam back to our upper hatch bubble. "You may wish to take hold of something solid," he advised.

"We're fine," Renzo said.

We were not fine. We had no idea what we were in for. The whale kicked its huge tail, surged forward, and yanked on the harnesses so hard that all three of us toppled to the floor. Renzo caught a flying bottle in the nick of time.

We made our way back to the viewing bubble, watching in delight as we zoomed through the dense curtain of bubbles trailing behind the whale. The craft shuddered and groaned and I probably should have been terrified, but it was simply too much fun for me to bother with fear.

For several miles we raced along. Then, without warning, the whale moved upward and so did we, as three screams came from three throats. The whale, to our amazement, breached. It shot clear out of the water and we followed, breaking into the too-bright air, flying through foam and sky before plunging back into the depths.

Deeper and deeper he dived as the three of us dropped to the floor. My body felt compressed by an invisible weight. Breathing was a struggle. I saw fear in the eyes of my friends as they, too, worked to find enough air.

"I can't breathe," I managed, gasping.

Tobble's eyes rolled up in his head and he stumbled around the craft, woozy, on the verge of fainting. I reached for him, but we bottomed out and turned back to the surface with such speed that I crashed against a bulkhead.

Then . . . peace. We fell into an uneasy calm, as the whale skimmed along the surface with us just below it.

All day and night it was more of the same: long stretches of gentle rocking motion, punctuated by dramatic plunges and leaps. We grew used to the moments of breathlessness, the sudden appearance of open sky, the astonishing, relentless speed.

The next morning, just as we were beginning to feel a

bit stir-crazy, Delgaroth entered our cabin and announced, "We approach Jaureggia, the great city and palace of Queen Pavionne."

I raced to the viewing bubble, ready for a change after so many leagues of ocean travel.

And what a change it was.

9

The Underwater Palace

"Look at that!" exclaimed Tobble, who'd squeezed up into the bubble with Renzo and me.

I don't know quite what I'd expected. I'd briefly visited an underwater natite hatchery, an impressive structure made of pink coral and gold stone. But that was a damp shack compared to this sprawling place. In size it was easily the equal of Saguria, the Murdano's capital city.

"Is that fire?" Renzo asked.

I followed the direction of his gaze and saw a long fissure in the seabed, one that glowed crimson as it emitted columns of furiously boiling water.

"Delgaroth mentioned they have a source of heat," I said. "Perhaps he meant something like that." We'd encountered lava from an ancient volcano once before. I had no desire to get near anything that hot ever again.

"I don't see any walls," Renzo observed. "No towers or gates, either. This city is wide open, if an enemy wanted to invade."

"Walls don't matter much in a world where everyone can easily swim over them," I said.

We were wrong to assume the city was defenseless, however. As we approached, a group of perhaps fifty natites swam to meet us, armed with spears and small crossbows strapped to their left arms. Some of the guards split off to swim toward the whale's head, while others gathered around Delgaroth, who was floating just outside our viewing hatch.

One of the natite soldiers peeked into the bubble, staring at us with an expression that was equal parts curiosity and astonishment.

"It's not every day they see a dairné, a wobbyk, and a human down here," I said.

"A dairne, a wobbyk, and a human." Renzo grinned. "Sounds like the beginning of a bad joke."

"Let's hope not," I replied.

The city encircled a fantastic structure that could only be Queen Pavionne's castle. At the center of the palace was the keep, a round tower that tapered as it rose. The top featured a tall spike with a viewing platform just below the sharp golden tip. I imagined natites swimming up there to observe the sunrises and sunsets, though I doubted that at this depth they could be as glorious as the one I'd witnessed earlier.

The entire palace showed no evidence of bricks or mortar.

In fact, as I looked at the castle and surrounding buildings—big homes and small, warehouses and shops—all were made of small, iridescent disks.

"Tarrick shells," Tobble said, as if he'd read my mind. "I'd heard stories that the natites could harness bivalves to grow as commanded."

"Those buildings are alive?" Renzo asked.

"Rather like the living coral walls we've seen in our travels," Tobble said.

The most astounding thing to me was not just the surreal architecture. It was how brightly illuminated the whole city seemed to be. There were shell-encased lanterns everywhere—on balconies, on poles, on the tops of buildings—all ablaze with a soft rosy light. Even here, far beneath the surface, the city glowed like a giant pink gem.

As we sank toward our landing spot, I caught sight of two markets filled with stalls. I recognized some familiar goods—things like bottles, pots, and knives—but many typical terrestrial items seemed to be missing. I saw no tethered goats or garilan carcasses, no chickens or horses for sale. Instead, the stalls teemed with cages full of living fish, seabeards, and halvids. Small mountains of shellfish, oysters, fillicks, clams, crabs, and pahdos shimmered in the pink light.

The whale who'd transported us dropped the harnesses, and our craft began to glide toward the lowest floor of the palace. A school of purple groupers swam close, nudging the barcabrena this way and that until we were aligned with a particular oval opening. We passed through the walls of the keep and found ourselves in a huge open space, with other similar craft arrayed in neat rows. With barely a bump, we came to a halt.

Delgaroth joined us in our compartment. "Are you ready?"

"I was born ready," Renzo said. "Who wouldn't want to jump out into water so deep that the top of the palace doesn't begin to reach the surface, eh?"

"As you were in the river, you'll be bubble-bound until we reach the air-breather meeting room, which has been made ready for you."

I exited the lower hatch, my heart thudding. Though I had plenty of air, I felt pressure on my chest, which made it hard not to panic. Natites swam freely in and out of open lattice-work walls, but despite that, the palace was not unguarded. Dozens of armed natites seemed to be stationed throughout.

As we progressed along a mirrored corridor, I was struck by the great variety of physical characteristics natites possessed. The only things they all seemed to have in common were four limbs and a head. The odd thing was that despite their webbed feet and hands, their gills and tentacles and extra set of translucent eyelids, they reminded me, more than anything, of humans.

"I wonder if natites and humans are related?" I mused aloud.

"Wait," said Renzo. "You think I look like . . . *him?*" He

jerked a thumb at Delgaroth.

"Yes and no," I said diplomatically.

"All living creatures are related," said Delgaroth, and I recalled Sabito's words after our eshwin hunt.

"True," said Renzo. "But still. I mean, let's start with the tentacles and work from there."

"Renzo," I cautioned under my breath, and he seemed to catch my warning.

Delgaroth was unfazed. "It's only surface creatures who deny the unity of life. Indeed," he added softly, "I suspect that is why you are here."

Why you are here. The pressure on my chest grew, and not because we were so far beneath the water. The potential for failure was enormous. My failure. Our failure.

I flashed on a memory of my visit to the Murdano's palace, another time I'd faced a daunting challenge with high stakes.

While there, I'd lied right to the Murdano's face.

It had come as a surprise to me that I *could* lie. Among dairnes, a species that instantly knows truth from deceit, lying is quite pointless.

And yet I'd done it. And lived to tell the tale.

In pursuit of truth, I'd lied to a tyrant.

In pursuit of peace, I'd joined an army.

Now I was in another palace, about to face a natite queen, tasked with determining the fate of countries on the brink of war.

It was dizzying, all the twists and ironies. Sometimes I felt like a bobbing piece of driftwood, carried along by an indifferent, rushing river.

Following Delgaroth, we entered a small room, not much more than a large box. A long pulley lifted us several stories until we reached what I took to be an anteroom, a sort of waiting area made of verrit shells layered with black volcanic glass. Into this space floated four large, well-armed soldiers and two elderly-looking natites, one of whom seemed to be half-overgrown with trailing weeds. Behind them was a young natite, petite in stature and covered in iridescent gold scales.

"When we meet, how shall I address the queen?" I asked Delgaroth.

He shot a startled glance toward the soldiers hovering behind him. "Queen Pavionne is not one for ceremony. It would be proper to refer to her as 'Your Majesty.' But she will not be offended if you forget."

"Is she a head-chopping sort of ruler, or does she just chain people in dungeons?" Renzo inquired, nudging me with his elbow.

"Pavionne seldom chops heads."

The answer came from the small natite in the rear, who, unnoticed by me, had moved closer.

As had the guards.

"That's a relief," Renzo said. "I don't much like any kind of royalty, but I like the head-chopping kind even less."

"You dislike royalty?" asked the golden natite.

"People who think they're better than everyone else just because of who their parents were?" Renzo laughed. "The kind of folks who assume they deserve the whole world on a platter, without ever doing a day's honest work?"

"Renzo," I murmured. I cleared my throat. Loudly.

"Surely not all royal rulers are like that!" said the golden natite.

"Pff," Renzo said, ignoring my pointed looks. "Once they have power, it goes right to their heads."

The natite nodded. "It can, yes. But a wise ruler, knowing the temptations of power, will resist it and devote herself to her people."

"Yeah, I'd like to see that sometime," Renzo continued as I covered my face with my hand. "But in my experience, people with power just spit on those like me."

The natite smiled. "I won't spit on you."

"Nah, of course you won't, you're just a—"

I watched the truth dawn on his face.

"A . . . ?" the natite pressed politely.

Renzo looked at me. He gulped.

"Your Majesty," I said, for of course the young natite was Queen Pavionne herself. "I beg your forgiveness for my companion's, um, hasty words."

My first act of diplomacy.

10
Conversation with a Queen

Queen Pavionne turned her confident gaze on me, and I caught my breath. She was a beautiful, shimmering creature, with spring-green eyes and a playful grin.

"I might have to chop off his head," Queen Pavionne said to me. And then she winked.

A natite queen *winked*. At *me*.

"While it's true that Renzo seldom uses his head," I replied, "I'd be grateful if you left it on his shoulders."

The queen laughed gaily. The sound was lilting, but it was hard not to be distracted by the sight of her teeth. They looked nothing at all like the teeth of a human, and a great deal like the teeth of a shark.

"May I present my friend?" I said. "Tobble of the wob-byks."

"Your Majesty." Tobble attempted a bow.

"A wobbyk! My goodness, I am glad to meet you," said the queen. "I have long said that if all sailors were wobbyks, we'd have no disputes with air-breathers. Yours is a wonderfully kind and polite species, and one that cares deeply for the sea."

Tobble's eyes grew so large his face almost disappeared. "Your Majesty, you are too kind."

"Come," Queen Pavionne said. "We're going up there." She pointed to a round hole in the ceiling. "Take my hand, friend Tobble. Ambassador Byx, my guards will carry you aloft. As for you, my opinionated human," she added, looking at Renzo with a falsely threatening expression, "they will carry you as well. Just as soon as they chop off your head."

It was a joke, of course, but while the queen was lighthearted, her guards were not. Not even a little bit. I didn't have the slightest doubt that if we threatened their ruler, the burly natites would remove our heads in short order.

Two of those guards seized me by the elbows, gently but with great strength. Two more took hold of Renzo. Tobble, clutching the hand of the queen, glanced back at us and sent a look that said: Can you believe this?

The hole in the ceiling was much like the barcabrena hatch. As soon as my head poked through, I found myself in dry air. Queen Pavionne, who was already standing in the room with Tobble, took my hand and hauled me the rest of the way. Renzo heaved himself up, not an easy task with the heavy burlap-camouflaged shield on his back. Ambassador Delgaroth arrived last, and the guards remained behind when the queen waved them off.

"Oh, I have to sit!" Queen Pavionne said. "I find standing in the dry tiring. I don't know how you do it. It makes you feel so heavy!"

I've had little experience of palaces, let alone of queens. I'd expected, given the size and opulence of the palace, to be taken to some impossibly grand and overwhelming chamber, with a gaudy throne for the queen, although natites rarely sit.

Here, not a throne was in sight. The queen flopped into one of half a dozen simple stone chairs. The contrast with the grandiose excess of the Murdano's palace was shocking.

Queen Pavionne shared something with Khara, I realized. Neither of them needed the outer trappings of rank to seem regal.

"So, Ambassador Byx. You know Delgaroth, of course." She nodded to the ambassador, who stood to her right side.

"The ambassador has been very good to us," I said.

Did I need to call her "Your Majesty" every two seconds? She seemed so approachable. Could I just talk to her like a normal person?

She's not a normal person, I reminded myself sternly. She's a powerful queen. Don't be gullible. Listen for lies. You have a job to do.

I cleared my throat. "Your Majesty, I bring greetings from the Lady of Nedarra, who—"

"Yes! Tell me about this Lady. We have often had . . . issues . . . with the Murdano, as we did with his father before him. We are intrigued by this new force rising on the surface world."

I noted she was using the royal "we," a reminder, perhaps, that we had come to the important part of our meeting.

"The Lady of Nedarra is brave and true," I answered. "She can be ruthless in a fight. But she is fair, honest, and righteous. She—"

"We like her already," the queen interrupted. "And clearly you do as well."

"I would give my life in an instant for Khara—for the Lady," I said, my throat swelling with emotion.

"As would we all," said Renzo, and Tobble nodded, paw over his heart.

The queen cupped her chin—or what would have been a chin in a human—in her thinly webbed hand. "And this Army of Peace of hers has but one goal?"

"To stop war between Dreyland and Nedarra," I said. "To

allow their peoples—all peoples—to live in peace and freedom."

The queen stared at me for what seemed like an unnervingly long time. At last she stood. "We have a message for the Lady of Nedarra. Shall we speak it to you?"

"Please, Your Majesty," I said, and I took a steadying breath.

Listen, Byx. Listen. Remember every word. I was glad to have Tobble and Renzo with me, so that they could fill in any holes in my recollection when we returned to Khara.

"Thus say I," the queen began, and I noticed she had dropped the formal "we." "I, Pavionne, natite Queen, to Kharassande Donati, now styled the Lady of Nedarra. Like you, I am young. Like you, I am a female of my species. Like you, I wish only for peace."

She paused, then added with a small smile, "Of course, everyone *says* they want peace. I suppose that is one advantage of having a dairne for an ambassador. Perhaps that is why the Lady sent you?"

"Perhaps," I agreed.

"I do not speak for all natites," the queen continued, "although I speak for most. My realm spreads from what you call the port of Velt, to the Nedarran Bay of Scales, and a thousand miles east into the great ocean. But within my realm, I wish friendly relationships with both Nedarra and

Dreyland. I know that both lands have corrupt leaders and that they plan war."

I nodded. "Indeed, it is imminent."

"Know that with every battle on the surface, dead bodies rain down upon my realm. I have no favorites. I am on no side but the side of my people." Her voice grew resolute. "But I will do all in my power to stop this war. My only goal is the happiness of my people."

"The Lady will be pleased to learn this," I said.

"Of course, my commitment to this cause will come at a small cost."

I'd been waiting for this moment. I was relieved to have the jeweled crown in my pouch, and the Subdur shield strapped to Renzo's back. It wasn't much, but it might afford us some leverage. "And the cost for your support will be?" I asked.

The queen was prepared. "A small amount of iron," she said, ticking items off on her fingers. "Also, some decorative pottery. I do love Nedarran ceramics. So colorful! Also, ownership of two tiny, unoccupied islands in the bay south of Saguria."

I blinked. Iron made sense. And even pottery, I supposed. "Why those particular islands?" I asked. They had no strategic importance, as far as I knew.

The queen shrugged, which, when tentacles are involved,

takes on a whole new meaning. "This may sound odd," she said, her voice falling back into its casual, light tone. "But you know how humans and lizards like to sun themselves? Lie around on warm rocks or on a sandy beach? We natites enjoy short periods in the open air. Isn't that right, Delgaroth?"

He blinked at the mention of his name. "It is quite true, Your Majesty. I find sunbathing most relaxing."

"We'd like to use the two islands for recreation," the queen explained.

"Recreation." I said it slowly, listening for undertones in her voice, or misdirection in her words. Strangely enough, I sensed no subterfuge. It seemed to be an entirely straightforward request.

"I have no doubt that the Lady of Nedarra will be willing to negotiate this in good faith," I said, trying to sound confident. "Your requests seem most reasonable."

"I'm so pleased," said the queen. And while her words rang true enough, I felt uneasy. It wasn't that she was lying. It was that something more was coming.

I glanced over at Renzo and Tobble. I could see they shared my doubt. Would it be wise to present the crown and shield now, as a token of our good faith? It was what Khara had directed. Still, the Army of Peace needed every last coin we could wrangle. And it was clear that Queen Pavionne's realm was wealthy beyond measure.

I tried to listen to my gut, but all I heard was a vague whine of hunger. It was different when I used my dairne instincts to sense a lie. Those answers came to me with certainty, the same way you know if you are hot or cold, happy or sad.

But this required a leap of judgment. And like that dark lake from my childhood, leaps into the unknown made me nervous.

I reached into my pouch to retrieve the crown. "Your Majesty, the Lady of Nedarra sends these small tokens of her commitment to your mutual cause."

My hand trembled as I extended the crown, and the queen gasped. I nodded to Renzo. "We bring you this great shield as well."

Renzo unwrapped the shield from its burlap covering and placed the heavy object at Queen Pavionne's feet.

"These are magnificent gifts," said the queen, holding up the crown to examine. "I know them well. The Crown of Beleeka and the Ganglid Shield." She placed the crown on her head, where it sat rather precariously. "They were stolen from this very castle by a traitorous band of rebels. They called themselves the Subdurs."

"Um . . . yes," I said. "That is, in fact, their provenance."

"Should I ask how they came into your possession?" asked

the queen, a hint of mischief in her tone.

"That is rather a long story," I answered.

"Filled with derring-do," Renzo added, and the queen rolled her eyes.

"There was a magical tube, too," Tobble said, "that I named a 'Far-Near.' Or was it a 'Near-Far'? It made near things seem close, and far things seem . . . No, wait! It was the other way around." His ears drooped a little. "Anyway. We had to give it away."

"Ah, well," said Queen Pavionne, smiling kindly at Tobble. "Please send my deepest gratitude for the return of these precious items. They mean a great deal to my people."

"So," I said, feeling relieved, "we are in agreement, it seems. I shall convey your requests to the Lady. Iron, pottery, and the two islands."

The queen laughed. "There's more, Ambassador Byx. Those were the small items. The appetizers, as it were, to get a sense of how forthcoming you might be."

So there *was* more at stake. I squared my shoulders, trying to look intimidating—something, to this day, I have yet to actually accomplish.

"I see," I said, as another wave of self-doubt washed over me. Had I misread her intent? "And what is it you *really* want?"

Queen Pavionne moved closer. I could tell she was considering her words with care. At last she put her hand on my shoulder.

"Ambassador Byx, come with me. I have a story I would like to tell. And a whale I would like you to meet."

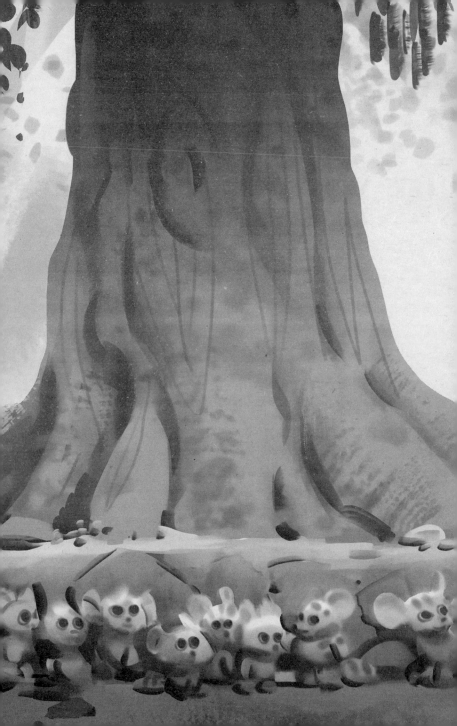

PART TWO
VOICE

11
Queen Pavionne's Demand

"Well, you obviously made a very good impression on the natite queen," said Khara. Four days had passed since my meeting with Queen Pavionne. We were gathered in Khara's tent: Renzo, Dog, Tobble, Gambler, Maxyn, and I. Sabito perched on a camp chair just inside the tent flap. Like most raptidons, he avoided enclosed spaces.

The Army of Peace had moved west along the Telarno during the brief time we'd been gone, as it attempted to gather more recruits. All along the route, the common folk—mostly human, but with a scattering of felivets and raptidons as well—had joined the cause. Delgaroth had returned us, loaded down with gifts for Khara, to the latest campsite.

Khara held up a bulky chalice. "This cup is solid gold and encrusted with jewels."

Renzo held up an index finger. "There's more where that

came from." He spread out his cloak and dumped a large sack onto it. Jewels glittered in green, azure, deep red, and startling pink.

Khara gasped. Even Gambler snorted in disbelief.

"These stones are enough for us to feed and arm our soldiers for months," said Khara.

I nodded. "Yes, that's exactly what the queen said."

"The shield went over very well." Renzo fingered a particularly large blue stone. "And Pavionne loved the crown."

"Pavionne?" Khara repeated, raising an eyebrow at Renzo.

"*Queen* Pavionne," Renzo amended.

"Our gifts were mere baubles compared to all this," said Khara. She leaned back, arms crossed over her chest. "I take it, then, that she supports our plan?"

I nodded. "In return, she'd like some iron, some Nedarran pottery, and two minor islands in the bay off Saguria."

"That's nothing." Khara narrowed her eyes. "There must be more."

"As it happens, yes." I stood and moved to the center of the tent. I wasn't sure why. In my role as ambassador, it felt appropriate, especially given what I had to say.

"This is a bit complicated," I began. "Tobble and Renzo will help me if my memory fails."

Khara nodded and gave me an encouraging smile.

"As you know, it has long been a mystery how natites are

able to communicate almost instantly across vast distances. When a human pays the natite tax in far-off Bossyp, how is it that the natites in the Chrisherna Sea seem to know it? How are they able to talk to each other in this way? To know what a fellow natite, one they've never met, knows?"

"I will say this," Gambler interjected. "If it's theurgy, it's like no theurgy ever practiced by human, felivet, raptidon, or terramant. During my time on the Isle of Scholars, this ability to communicate was one of the mysteries I studied. Natites there would reveal nothing."

"It isn't theurgy," Renzo said flatly. "I saw it being done. I would have known if magic was involved."

"Saw what being done?" Khara asked. "How? By whom?"

"Whales," I said.

Khara frowned. "Whales?"

"Whales," I repeated. "Sailors know that whales vocalize."

"Oh, yes indeed!" Tobble exclaimed. "They sing! It's quite a sound!"

"A sound," I continued, "that acts very differently in water than it does in air. The songs the whales make aren't just heard by those nearby. They reverberate for hundreds of miles."

Khara gave a short, sharp laugh. "Am I supposed to believe that natites can communicate with whales? Natites are one of the governing species. Whales are, well, just animals."

I shook my head. "I sensed no dishonesty at all from the queen when she told us . . . well, when she said something you will find hard to believe."

"Go on," said Khara.

"Natites are whales," I began. "And whales are natites. I don't mean they're exactly the same thing, but to natites, whales are close relations. Family, even. They call the whales brothers and sisters, fathers and mothers. The natites believe they came from whales. That over vast stretches of time, some whales changed, so much so that they were no longer true whales, but a whole new thing: natites."

I paused and took a breath. Who would have guessed that being an ambassador involved so much speaking? Meanwhile, Khara waited, expressionless. I couldn't tell if she was doubtful, annoyed, or intrigued.

"When the queen told us this, she knew we would be skeptical, so she demonstrated," I continued. "She asked me to name a kind of water creature. I chose a squid. The queen started to . . . sing, I suppose you'd call it. It was a brief song, a sort of slow, undulating vibration." I paused. "In less time than it takes to fry an oatcake—"

"Very little time," Tobble interrupted. "You want to be careful not to overcook an oatcake."

"As I was saying," I went on, "in less time than—"

"Three minutes on one side, just one minute on the other side, or the oatcake will . . ." Tobble trailed off. "Um, never mind. I apologize for the interruption. It was rude of me. Carry on."

"In the very little time it takes to fry an oatcake," I said, "a small whale appeared out of the depths."

"If by 'small,' you mean very, very big," Renzo added.

"On the queen's command," I said, "he opened his mouth and displayed, within his cavernous jaw, a large, very annoyed squid."

Khara sat perfectly still. I knew it wasn't because she didn't understand my story, but because she did. This was a power beyond the ability of any human, felivet, raptidon, terramant, or dairne. It was beyond theurgy.

No one stirred as this new reality sank in, although Renzo and Tobble and I had already spent our return trip grappling with the revelation. If it was possible to communicate over vast distances, then natites had a power to rival that of dairnes. A power that tyrants like the Murdano and the Kazar Sg'drit would fear.

Tyrants have no greater fear than the truth. And if the truth could be known quickly, and by all? What then?

Khara spoke at last, her voice oddly subdued. "And what does Queen Pavionne ask of me?"

"She asks that if you bring down the Murdano, *when* you bring down the Murdano, the ruler who comes next will agree to have a natite present at all council meetings."

Gambler shifted uneasily. "And tell the whole wide natite

world what this new ruler is saying and doing?"

"Yes," I said. "The next ruler must rule openly, in plain view of all species. No secrets. That's Queen Pavionne's demand."

Khara gave a curt nod. "And in exchange?"

"In exchange, she will ensure that you are never without money to buy weapons or feed your troops. And she will stop the Murdano's navy from attacking Dreyland."

Khara didn't have to utter a word. I already knew her answer.

Later, as the others headed back to their tents, Khara motioned for me to stay. "Byx," she said, "I want to thank you for your service. You accomplished everything we'd hoped. I'll send a messenger to communicate my decision to the queen."

Dairnes don't blush, of course, but we do get embarrassed. Beneath the fur on my face, I could feel a rush of heat. "I'm relieved it went well," I said. "I was so afraid I'd let you—all of us—down."

"That, my friend, will never happen." Khara clapped me on the back.

"I hope you're right."

We stepped outside her tent into the damp, chill air. Khara's guard, a young female human, snapped to attention. "We've completed our first challenge, Byx," said Khara.

"Now comes the next step. We'll discuss it more at the war council convening in a few days. But first I need to know: Are you game for more?"

Flushed with pride at Khara's praise, at that moment I felt invincible. "Ready and willing," I replied.

It was only later that night, lying awake on my cot as I watched the moon turn tree limbs into grasping shadows, that my doubts resurfaced.

I was ready to help. I wanted to do my part. But was I really *able*? Able to do all that Khara would be asking of me?

Sleep eluded me that evening, and many more evenings to follow. Some nights, even with Tobble snoring soundly nearby, only the silent moon listened to my fears.

12
The War Council

I'd never been to a war council before. Until Khara had said it, I'd never even heard the phrase "war council." And I'd certainly never expected to attend one.

Let alone speak to it.

But there I was.

The council convened six days after our return from Jaureggia, in a clearing at the center of our latest camp. Khara's generals and chief advisers were there, including Bodick the Blue and General Varis, along with other allies, all of whom had been en route to join the army even before my visit to Queen Pavionne.

Mysenie Marrak, a quiet, capable fellow, delivered a force of five hundred archers armed with formidable bows, all the way from the southern reaches of the Forest of Null.

An ancient, gray-bearded ally named Feldrick, a supposed

criminal from the Therian Marshes, came too. He'd been outlawed for fighting back when the Murdano's soldiers had tried to slaughter his entire village. Feldrick had brought three hundred men and women, mostly ax-wielding people who called themselves "Marshcats."

A strange man named Woad was also in attendance, along with one hundred warriors from the western slopes of the Perricci Mountains. Woad and his fighters wore leather jerkins and strange pointed shoes. His entire face, neck, and shoulders were covered in black tattoos designed to make him look half human, half felivet, although Gambler was decidedly unimpressed.

Arriving by sky was a broad-winged green-and-red raptidon named Stimball, an adviser to Rorid Headcrusher, a mighty raptidon leader.

Gambler, Renzo, Sabito, Tobble, and Maxyn completed the group. Maxyn had recovered sufficiently to be able to walk without his crutch for brief periods, though I could tell he was still in a lot of pain.

In all, we were two dozen or so, standing in a circle around a table set up in the open air. The sky was busy with dark, roaming clouds, and the temperature was dropping, though it was only noon. The air held the sharp smell of advancing rain.

A large, frayed map lay on the table, held down by stones at each corner. It showed all of Nedarra, the southern reaches of Dreyland, and a sliver of far-off Marsony.

"To begin with, General Varis will lay out the problem," Khara said. "Then I will hear your advice." She smoothed the center of the map. "Wise Varis points out that all wars involve reading the land. Rivers, mountains, seacoast, forests: these are what we must understand. General?"

She stood back and the grim-faced general stepped up. His battered sword looked like it had seen a thousand battles. And perhaps it had.

"To our north, the Sovo Ridge divides us from Dreyland," he began. "But we know that the Kazar Sg'drit has enthralled terramants and forced them to dig a great tunnel beneath those mountains. His plan is to open the tunnel and deliver terramant shock troops onto the plains south of Zebara, followed by his army. They will ravage the area, burn crops and villages, kill livestock and people. But after that, they'll run into the Perricci Mountains, which will stand between them and the Murdano's capital of Saguria."

I watched his thick index finger trace a route on the map. I didn't know the geography nearly as well as most, but this much, at least, I understood.

"From the Zebaran plains, the Dreylanders have two choices. They can scale the Perricci Mountains and follow the southern edge of the range into Saguria. Or they can send their forces, both human and terramant, down the coast, which means passing through a dense forest and crossing a river. The Murdano will have fortified that path. It would be a long, bloody fight to reach Saguria, let alone take the city."

I had the odd realization that I didn't know which side to support in that battle. I'd been born in Nedarra, of course. But I certainly owed nothing to the murderous Murdano.

General Varis stroked his red beard, studying the map. "I believe if they break out from the terramant tunnels, the Kazar will send his troops over the Perricci Mountains. Since the Murdano doesn't know about the tunnels, he won't have strongly fortified the Zebaran plains or the mountains. Still, it would be a hard crossing in cold weather for the Dreylanders. Many would die from the sickness that comes with climbing too high."

"Ah, I've heard of that," Tobble whispered in my ear.

I couldn't help but notice smug looks from both Sabito and Stimball at the very idea that altitude might make one sick.

Woad spoke, and it was the first time I'd heard his voice, surprisingly high-pitched for such a wild-looking creature.

"We're accustomed to great heights. And we know the Perricci Mountains, which we call the Goldanvaal, like we know the faces of our own children. However difficult that path is for the Dreylanders"—he pounded his chest with his fist—"we can make it much, much harder."

Khara nodded. "I was hoping you would volunteer, Woad."

"We would wish to get our children and others who cannot fight to a safe place first," Woad added.

"Of course."

"But then?" He grinned, which was not a reassuring look, given his tattoos and missing teeth. "It would be like going home. Those are our mountains! We get jumpy down here in the flatlands."

"What if I told you," said Khara, "that I would have you do all you can to delay the Dreylanders crossing the Perriccis without attacking them?"

Woad laughed. "I'd be sorry not to plant my ax in a few Dreylander skulls. But truth be told, we can delay them more easily by felling trees, diverting streams, and causing landslides. Blocking roads and paths would make life miserable for them."

It was clear that Woad liked the idea. He was practically rubbing his hands together with glee.

"We are ready to help as well," said Stimball, the raptidon. "The eagles of Gore's Peak, the highest mountain in the Perriccis, will act as your eyes in the sky, Woad."

"Hah!" Woad exclaimed. "And glad we shall be of your help, friend raptidon."

Gambler cleared his throat.

"Yes, Gambler?" Khara asked.

"The Kazar Sg'drit is a valtti, a rogue felivet. He is cunning. I believe he will have a second line of attack."

"That would be the wise thing to do," said General Varis. "The Murdano's army is large, but not so large that it can be everywhere, all the time. And what army can stand against a thousand or more terramants and well-trained troops?"

"If the natite queen does as she's promised and stops the Murdano's navy," Khara said, pacing back and forth, "we'll have ensured an eventual Dreylander victory. We will have traded one tyrant for another. And that is not our goal."

Bodick the Blue spoke up. "Once the terramants break through with their tunnel, a wave of them will pour into the Zebaran plains." Despite her intense gaze, her voice was calm and soothing. "We'll do what we can to stop them, but that leaves dozens of villages, thousands of farms, and tens of thousands of innocent people to the mercy of the terramants and the Kazar."

"To stop them at the tunnel," said Khara, "we would have to get there first—and that we cannot do."

Everyone was quiet for a few minutes. We stared at the map as if we could force a solution to appear by sheer will. The wind picked up, and around us tents fluttered like sheets drying on a line.

"Um . . . I'm not exactly a general. I'm just a thief," Renzo said. He sounded uncertain, even shy, which was not at all like him. "But couldn't we send a smaller group ahead to at least delay the terramant attack? If we slow them down, they'll cause less mischief among innocent villagers. And they'll be in all the greater hurry to cross the Perriccis, where Woad's people can delay them again."

"With my people to act as guides," Woad answered, "we could perhaps get a small force near the tunnel openings, but it could take weeks to get those soldiers into place." He scratched the back of his head. "They would get there ahead of the Lady's army, but not by much."

Renzo sighed, slowly nodding.

Stimball waved a wing. "Raptidons could cross the mountains in that time, but we cannot defeat terramants, or even delay them by much. When we fight alongside ground dwellers, we are effective. But on our own?"

Tobble timidly raised a paw, but no one noticed except me.

"Can we raise the local people to fight?" Bodick asked.

General Varis shrugged. "Farmers. And with what weapons? Pitchforks and hoes? Against terramants and the troops of the Kazar?"

"Bodick's right," said Khara. "We need reinforcements."

Tobble waved his paw with more force. No one paid him any mind, but I was curious. "Yes, Tobble?" I said.

"I, um—" He looked around, tongue-tied, at the circle of warriors.

"Go ahead, Tobble," Khara said. "Please."

"What if raptidons could carry fighters over the mountains?" Tobble asked, his huge ears trembling.

"You give us too much credit," said Sabito. "You think a raptidon could carry someone the size of, say, General Varis?"

The group broke into laughter, and at first I thought Tobble might retreat and fall silent. But Sabito's scorn seemed to spur on my little friend.

"Of—of—of course you couldn't carry a human or a felivet," Tobble said. "But, meaning no reproach—we are all friends here, and I apologize if my words offend either of you admirable raptidons—but . . . well. Raptidons have certainly carried wobbyks away. And I think the largest raptidons might even carry a dairne."

Woad laughed again, but Khara did not. "What are you suggesting, Tobble?" she asked, leaning forward.

"My lady, we are a small people, we wobbyks, and often dismissed as inferior since we are not a governing species. But you have seen that when we are angry enough, we can be, well, very impolite."

This time Khara did laugh, and so did I.

"Impolite?" she echoed. "*Impolite?* I've seen you in action, my friend. The word 'ferocious' is more apt."

"However fierce friend Tobble may be," Bodick said, "he is only one small wobbyk."

Tobble turned to Bodick. "What if there were five hundred of me?"

Woad began to speak, but Khara silenced him with a slight motion of her hand. "Five hundred? Where would we find five hundred wobbyks ready to risk their lives?"

As it happened, Tobble had an answer for that.

13
Two Small Creatures

"I'm sorry to be sending you off again, Byx," Khara said the following morning while we ate our breakfast of porridge and rashers, "but you're too valuable to waste, just lying around camp."

Did I puff up a little at the word "valuable"? Yes, I admit that I did.

"Of course, you'll once more carry the title of 'ambassador,'" Khara added.

Did I deflate a little at the word "ambassador"? Perhaps a bit.

I was beginning to suspect that while titles can be impressive, they can also be a prison. Once you acquire a label, certain things are expected of you.

Truth was, despite Khara's praise, I still felt a little like a fraud. An imposter. "Ambassador" continued to ring false to my ears. Perhaps it always would.

Nonetheless, I knew my mission to the natite queen had helped the Army of Peace. I hadn't disappointed Khara, or my friends, or, most importantly, myself.

And if Khara wanted me to continue as ambassador, then so be it.

It was early, chilly and damp. The threatened rain had come and gone during the night. With some help from Renzo, I'd packed my saddlebags with food and warm blankets. Two waterskins hung on leather straps. Havoc even had new horseshoes, courtesy of a blacksmith who'd joined the army.

Khara had given me a small drawstring bag of natite jewels, and Renzo was busy casting a theurgic spell over the bag. Supposedly, it would make it hard for people to see the jewels unless I wanted them to be seen.

"Are you sure you know how to do that?" Khara asked Renzo, secretly winking at Tobble and me.

"What?" Renzo demanded. "You dare question my ability to cast concealing spells on jewels? May I remind you that this is my area of expertise?"

"I suppose it takes a thief to hide things from thieves," Tobble said. "Not that I meant to call you a thief," he added hastily. "I would never wish to insult you!"

Renzo reached down and hoisted Tobble behind me on my saddle. "Tobble, I *am* a thief."

"You *were* a thief," Khara said.

"Yes, I was a thief," Renzo said with a wistful sigh. "Now I'm a horse trader."

"What do you mean, Renzo?" I asked as I adjusted a stir-rup.

"The Lady Khara is sending me to the Infina to purchase horses." He said "purchase" with obvious distaste.

"Yes, purchase," Khara said. "I've entrusted a large number of jewels to you, ex-thief Renzo."

Renzo finished settling Tobble in place, positioning tiny stirrups so he could sit more comfortably behind me. Khara stepped close when Renzo turned to her. Quite close, in fact. I noticed Gambler looking away, his eyes smiling, though his face was, as always, intimidating.

"What makes you think I won't take the jewels and buy myself a nice farm somewhere safe?"

"You won't," Khara said.

"You seem very sure," Renzo said.

Khara touched his cheek and left her fingers there for what seemed—to me, at least—a long time. Renzo bowed his head and for a moment their foreheads touched. It was not the sort of thing a great lady would do with a thief. Nor was it the kind of thing a thief would dare with a great lady.

"Oh!" I exclaimed, but quietly, so that only Tobble and Gambler heard me.

"I believe," Tobble said, looking at Gambler, "that Byx

just figured something out."

Gambler nodded. "I believe you're right."

Both of them seemed amused. Clearly I was the last to see what seemed obvious, now that I thought about it: the Lady and the thief were in love.

I thought of my mother and father. I'd often seen them looking at each other like they were the only two dairnes in the world. It was the single example of love—that kind of love—I'd ever witnessed. Somehow, in my innocent way, I'd imagined that it was only my mother and father who looked at each other that way.

Khara and Renzo?

"I am a little slow sometimes," I confessed.

"They are of the age for that sort of thing," said Gambler. The fur on his shoulders rippled in a sort of felivet shrug. I suspected he didn't disapprove of Khara and Renzo so much as the idea of romance itself. Felivets are solitary animals, for the most part.

"You're going with Renzo?" I asked Gambler.

"I am," he said. "I would happily go with you, Byx, but the people you are going to see are not fond of my kind."

"Perhaps because your kind eats my kind," Tobble said.

"Yes," Gambler said, "that may be it."

While Renzo saddled his own horse, Khara came to me, checking every last detail of my pack. When she was satisfied, she said, "Byx, I am sending you and Tobble alone because I think two small creatures on a small horse may not attract the eyes of soldiers looking for trouble."

"Yes." I forced a smile. "We'll be fine."

Khara looked at the two of us, the dairne and the wobbyk, and nodded. "You two are unlikely heroes, maybe, but I believe in you."

I heard Tobble stifle a sob.

"Now, listen to me," Khara said, dropping her voice. "This is the second part of your mission, Byx. I have complete faith in you. But you've been through much in your short life. I worry for you and Tobble sometimes. I don't know what lies ahead, but we are on the precipice of war, and war changes people. I want you to stay true to what you believe. Whatever comes, remember who you are."

"Yes, my lady," I said, suddenly formal, even as I wondered again if the old Byx even existed anymore.

"Sabito and Stimball are flying to friendly rookeries to gather support. They will meet you to help transport the wobbyks you'll have recruited."

"You sound so confident," I said.

"That's because I am."

I heard a clattering of hooves. General Varis charged up on his horse, a chestnut beast twice the size of Havoc.

"Good, you haven't left yet." He swung down out of his saddle—quite gracefully, given his size—and retrieved something from a leather bag. "I have a gift."

He unwrapped a fabric covering to reveal a small, tear-drop-shaped shield made of wood and boiled leather.

"It should be about your size, Byx," said the general. "You hold it like this." He mimed slipping an arm through the straps. He couldn't very well stick his actual arm through, as it was the size of my two legs put together. "The round part at the top covers your body. The pointed part at the bottom will protect your legs if you are riding."

"That is very kind of you, General," I said. "Thank you. I have no way to repay you."

"Yes, you do," he said, returning to his usual warrior self. "Accomplish the mission the Lady has given you and I shall be more than repaid."

I attempted a salute, like I'd seen some of the soldiers do. He returned it. At which point Tobble decided he'd better salute, too, although he ended up poking himself in the eye.

We rode away, yelling our goodbyes, feeling hopeful, excited, and fearful all at once.

14
Goodbye to Maxyn

We hadn't gone far when, just outside the camp, I saw Maxyn standing alone.

"Maxyn!" I called. "Are you waiting for someone?"

"For you." He offered a hesitant smile. "Of course."

I dismounted so he wouldn't have to gaze up at me. And because I sensed he wished to speak privately.

"It's good to see you walking more," I said.

"I still need my crutch from time to time. But I am definitely improved. Enough, it seems, that I, too, have a mission to perform for the Lady."

"Oh?" I said. It surprised me to hear that Khara would assign work to Maxyn so soon. But she needed to use every talent at her disposal, and dairnes like Maxyn and me did, after all, have a unique ability.

"I'm to board a small ship at the mouth of the Telarno."

"A ship?" I asked. "We have a ship?"

"No, but there's a pirate ship."

"What? You're going away with pirates?"

"These pirates have made trouble for themselves with the natites," he explained. "They're extremely interested in getting back into Queen Pavionne's good graces. The Lady says we'll be watched closely by unseen natite eyes."

I touched his shoulder. "But where are you going?"

"To the lost colony," he said. "I'm to sail clear around Nedarra to the Pellago River. I'm not well enough to ride a horse for any great distance."

I frowned. The lost colony was a tiny, isolated dairne fishing village. "Does Khara expect you to bring dairnes to the fight?"

"No. I think the Lady understands I'm no warrior." Maxyn threw up his hands. "She's looking ahead to the hoped-for peace. She doesn't seek dairne swords. She seeks dairne truth telling."

I gazed at my fellow dairne, my gentle mirror. "I'm sorry to be leaving you, Maxyn. I wish we'd had more time to become better friends."

I wasn't quite sure what I meant. Had I hoped Maxyn would become as dear to me as Tobble? Or was I talking about the way Khara and Renzo were friends?

Gambler had said the two humans were of the age for things like romance. But I didn't think I was. And in any case,

I didn't seem to feel that way about Maxyn.

Still, our connection was unique. We were two dairnes in a world with far too few of our kind remaining. After the slaughter of my family and village, I'd traveled Nedarra convinced I was an endling until the moment I'd seen Maxyn and his father. That memory would be etched in my heart forever.

"I fear you have the harder path ahead, Byx. I'll be lolling about the ship, lying in the sun and dining every night on fresh fish." He looked over his shoulder, making sure Tobble couldn't overhear. "The thing is, I . . ."

"What's wrong, Maxyn?"

"Nothing."

"It's all right. You can tell me."

"Byx, I'm not brave like you." His words poured out like tears. "Tell me how to do it. Tell me how *you* do it."

My mouth hung open. "I . . . I . . . What?"

"You went face-to-face with a Knight of the Fire. You stood before the Murdano without crumbling. You saved the dairne colony."

His last reference made me queasy. It had been my idea to float fire ships into a Marsonian blockade of the colony. Many—far too many—Marsonians had died because of me.

The old Byx would never have done such a thing.

"I was scared all the while," I admitted.

"You, scared?"

"Terrified," I said. And of course, being a dairne, Maxyn knew I spoke the truth. "I don't think you can stop being scared, Maxyn. I don't think that's what it means to be brave. I think being brave means being afraid and still doing what you must do."

Even, I added silently, if it means abandoning your childhood self. Even if it means becoming someone cold and calculating. Someone capable of rationalizing brutality in the service of a greater good.

"Perhaps," Maxyn said. He sounded dubious.

"Maxyn, whatever comes, remember who you are." I felt like a fraud, parroting words Khara had spoken to me just minutes earlier. But I'm no speechmaker. I didn't know how to sound inspiring.

Maxyn cocked his head, smiling shyly. "Do you ever wonder what will happen to us when all this"—he waved his hand toward the army encampment—"is over?"

"Not really," I admitted.

"Will we go to live with other dairnes?" Maxyn asked. "Start new colonies? New . . . families?"

"I suppose," I said. "But for now, this is my family. I guess I'm afraid to think that far ahead, you know?"

"Fare you well, Byx," Maxyn said, his dark eyes shimmering. He waved to Tobble. "And safe travels to you, friend Tobble!"

We embraced, a bit awkwardly. I climbed back into my

saddle and off we went. Every so often I turned back to see Maxyn, watching us disappear from view. I felt a stubborn lump in my throat and hot tears threatening.

Be resolute, I told myself. You'll see Maxyn again. You'll see all your friends soon enough.

In the meantime, I had a map. I had a small sword and a shield. I had jewels in my pouch. I had my faithful Havoc. And I had my dear friend Tobble.

All I had to do was something that had never been done before, knowing that the armies of two nations would happily see me dead.

"This will be fun," Tobble said, without any conviction whatsoever.

"An adventure," I said, my tone just as flat. "Though I don't like being separated from everyone."

Tobble nudged me with his nose. "You're not separated from me."

"You know what I mean, Tobble. Khara and the Army of Peace are in danger. We won't have any way of knowing what's happening to them until it's too late."

Tobble fell silent. Nothing he could say would comfort me, because we both knew I was right. We would simply have to tolerate the horrible uncertainty.

Of course, I reminded myself, that was true of all of life, wasn't it? I recalled something my father, who loved wise sayings and proverbs, used to say: "The only thing certain is uncertainty." How right he'd been.

We rode all day. For two hours we followed the Telarno north before turning westward into forested terrain toward our final goal, Bossyp.

I have some experience of forests now. And I can say that some are lovely, lush places, carpeted by fallen leaves and populated with docile creatures.

You get a feel for the character of a forest. Some of them almost seem to invite you in.

We were not entering one of those forests.

On the map, the stretch of dense trees had no name. But before we'd departed that morning, Bodick the Blue had taken Tobble and me aside.

"I argued with myself about whether to tell you this," she began, which was not an encouraging start. "I don't wish to frighten you, Byx. But I know things about the forest you'll be riding through. Things few others know."

Definitely not an encouraging start.

"There's a reason the forest isn't named on the map. You see, a very long time ago, before the flood, even before Urman's yew, there was a magician, a sorcerer. And you must understand that in those long-ago days, theurgy wasn't the weak force it is now, used only for small, temporary spells. Back then, magic was very powerful, and no magician was more powerful than"—Bodick looked around nervously—"than Gaziko. And the reason that no map shows the name of the forest is that its true name is Gaziko's Ezkutak."

"What a strange-sounding name," said Tobble.

"It's an ancient tongue, a language of evil." Bodick shuddered.

"But surely this magician is long dead?" I said. "Any spells would have faded by now, right?"

Bodick forced a doubtful smile. "I'm sure that's true," she said. "But I felt you should be told nonetheless."

Now, facing a phalanx of dark, enormous trees, we recalled Bodick's warning. But even without her words, I would have felt something wrong about the forest ahead.

Even before she'd told us that Ezkutak was the ancient word for *horror.*

"Centuries ago," Tobble muttered under his breath as we rode beneath the trees. "It was all centuries ago."

"Yes," I agreed, inhaling the dank odor of moss and decay. "Long, long ago. And it's a large forest, many square miles. Whatever this evil wizard did or didn't do, it would have been in some small part of the forest, not all of it."

"Of course," Tobble agreed.

On we went, trying to talk ourselves out of our fears.

But horses don't understand speech. They know only what they feel. And judging by his hesitant steps and low-hung head, Havoc didn't like this forest. Not at all.

And it turned out he was right.

15
Gaziko's Ezkutak

As we ventured into the gloomy forest, the trail petered out, and we were left to find our way on our own. As long as the sun remained in the sky, we knew our direction, but the days were growing ever shorter as winter approached. Once night fell, we wouldn't be able to see the stars through the dense canopy of tree limbs.

At the border of the forest, we'd faced tall, straight ever-greens with branches so high on the trunks that we could easily skirt most of them. But as we continued, the evergreens vanished, replaced by gnarled, misshapen oaks and drooping, black-leaved tyru trees.

We pressed on, knowing that every minute was precious if we were to accomplish our goal. But the darkness grew ever deeper, until I couldn't even see Havoc's nose.

I tried for a happy voice. "Well, I suppose we're going to

have to make camp here. The ground's flat and dry. And I hear a stream nearby. At least we'll be able to refill our water-skins."

"I don't like this place," Tobble said, clearly not fooled by my attempt at optimism.

"Come on, Tobble. Are we really going to be frightened by tales of long-gone evil?"

"Yes," Tobble said. "We definitely are."

"You'll feel better when we get a fire going. A nice little fire. That's what we need."

We found plenty of dead branches and fallen tree trunks, but it was so dark that we had to drop to all fours and feel around for each piece. An hour passed before we had a decent fire, and by that time we were both quite hungry.

Even with the fire going, we could see only a few feet in any direction. We ate in silence, listening to the stream gurgling. Finding it would have to wait for morning. When we'd finished eating, I hung a sack of oats over Havoc's head, and Tobble and I laid out our bedrolls.

Given my nerves, I didn't expect to fall asleep. For his part, Tobble vowed to stay alert all night. But after just a few minutes, I heard his familiar singsong snoring, and that sound, along with a hard day of riding, allowed my weariness to overcome fear.

The next morning, I woke with a start. Tobble was looking down at me, his hand on my shoulder. His eyes were even larger than usual. And he was trembling.

I blinked, adjusting to the sickly gray light. "What is it?" I asked.

Tobble couldn't speak. He could only stare.

I stood, and then I saw.

Not a hundred yards distant was a desolate clearing. At its center was a large mound, ten times my own height. A mound made completely of bones.

"It's some . . . some kind of . . . ," I began, but I had no idea what it was. What natural explanation could there be for this mountain of bones? And even if there was one, it wouldn't have explained what we saw next.

The trees surrounding us weren't simply trunks, branches, and leaves. Each and every tree had grown in and around and through skeletons.

Closest to us was what appeared to be a human skeleton several feet off the ground. A foot protruded through dark leaves. Out of a low branch, a bony hand seemed to point to the sky. When I focused my unwilling eyes, a skull stared vacantly back at me from just inside a deep cleft in the tree.

Tobble hugged my waist, his head half-buried in my fur.

"What is this place?" I asked in a strangled voice. "What kind of monster would have made it?"

"We can't . . . we can't . . . we can't go on!" said Tobble. "This is a cursed place!"

I put an arm around his shoulders, comforting him. But

I needed comforting as well, because Tobble was not wrong. This was an evil place.

"What was that?" Tobble yelped.

"What?" I demanded.

"I heard something. Like a whisper."

Dairnes have excellent hearing. But wobbyk ears are better still. Tobble's were quivering, aiming away to our left.

I waited. And then I heard it, too. A gravelly voice uttered what might have been a song or a poem:

> Great fools come, and great fools go,
> But none defy great Gaziko.
> He strips their flesh and bleaches bone,
> And for their insults they atone.
> Serve, obey him, grovel, praise,
> Or suffer greatly all your days.
> Thus shall it be: reap what you sow,
> For none defy great Gaziko.

We exchanged troubled looks. We both wanted nothing more than to escape this horrifying place. But there was something hypnotic in the simple verse, something that made us wish to see, need to see, its source.

In spite of ourselves, we walked in the direction of the song, which had begun to repeat.

Then, with disbelieving eyes, we saw it.

The head was set upon a wide tree stump. No body. No arms. Just a head and a neck fused into the ringed wood of an ancient tree. Green shoots twined from the stump, weaving around the neck.

It was not the head of a human, or a felivet, or any species I'd ever seen. It was hairless, its flesh bloodred and welted with raised orange stripes. Two vertical slashes mid-face widened and narrowed with each breath, though how it was breathing and where that breath could go, I dared not even guess.

What seemed to be a mouth formed a wide V, sharp at the bottom, a sort of grotesque smile. Two small eyes were slitted black, like the eyes of a serpent. Three twisting horns protruded from the top of the head.

We stood there, unblinking, unable to move, as the head ground out its foul yet childish rhymes.

He'll cut your flesh, you'll bleed a stream,
He'll gouge your eyes until you scream.
Near or far, where e'er you go,
You'll not escape great Gaziko.

"What is it?" Tobble whispered.

Slowly I shook my head. "I don't know, Tobble."

The eyes, which had been staring blankly ahead, jerked to focus on me.

A dairne, a wobbyk come to see,
What Gaziko has done to me.

A dairne. A wobbyk.

I froze, as Tobble clung to me like a life raft in a stormy sea.

"He sees us!" Tobble cried. "Byx, he sees us!"

16
Stump

Since the tragedy that had set me on my long journey, I'd seen many strange and frightening things. None, however, had been more bizarre than the sight confronting me now.

And yet, though the head was truly terrifying, something else was stirring inside me: pity.

Who could have done such a terrible thing to another living creature?

I wanted to recoil. I wanted to grab Tobble, leap atop Havoc, and gallop away.

But I couldn't.

I cleared my throat. "I would—" I began, before my voice turned to a mouselike squeak.

I tried again. "I would know your name, sir. Or madam. Or whatever."

My name is Stump, and you should know,
A name bestowed by Gaziko.
In deep-forgotten memory,
They called me Lord of Castle Rhee.

Tobble squeezed my arm so tightly it hurt. "But what manner of creature are you?" I asked the head.

A creature cursed through all of time,
To mutter naught but childish rhyme.
Once we were mighty Caddalites,
Now lonely bones to haunt the nights.

I looked back and could just make out the jumble of bones we'd seen. At first glance, I'd assumed by their size that they were human, but as I searched for detail, I noticed that all the skulls had horns.

"I think those are—were—his people," I said. "Caddalites. Isn't that what he called them?"

Tobble, still buried in my fur, peeked out long enough to say, "Ask him where his people are. Maybe we could let them know he's . . . like this."

"Stump?" I felt rude using that name, but it was the name he'd given us. "Where are your people?"

Stump blinked his reptilian eyes. His next words, though doggerel, struck deep.

The Caddalites once lived in peace,
In western lands we called Florbees.
Till Gaziko took all we knew,
Left only me to rhyme for you,

To tell the tale through all of time,
In endless verse and tortured rhyme,
A species lost, a living ghost.
A threat to all, an endling boast.

At the word "endling" I emitted a startled yelp. "What kind of monster would slaughter an entire species?" I demanded.

The weak and frightened long to kill,
The blood of innocents to spill.
'Tis ever easier to hate,
Than learn or love, or to create.

I am the endling of my race,
And never will I leave this place.
I speak unwilling poems just so
That all will fear great Gaziko.

I brushed tears from my eyes. There was nothing to do. Nothing we could change.

"I'm sorry," I whispered. "So sorry."

Stump closed his eyes and said no more.

We rode away in a far worse state than we'd arrived. An endling. I'd just come face-to-face with an endling. Perhaps I was seeing a nightmare vision of my own future.

For many miles, neither of us spoke. A terrible, cold weight had settled on our hearts, a sadness for the poor soul we'd left behind.

I wondered if anyone remembered the Caddalites. Was there some learned scholar who, on hearing the name, would light up and say, "Ah, yes, the Caddalites!" Or were Stump's people remembered only by the rare travelers who passed near enough to hear his ghastly rhymes?

How many centuries had he lived under this terrible spell? What sort of magician had powers so great that his spells and curses could last for generations?

And when at last the destroyers of this world—the Murdanos, the Kazars, all the greedy, reckless monsters—had killed the last of my kind, would there even be a Stump to mark our passing?

"How will we survive against such evil?" I said, not realizing I'd spoken aloud till Tobble answered.

"By not letting them win!" he snapped.

The residue of horror, like a poison in our veins, had made him speak harshly. But of course, being Tobble, he apologized profusely.

"What amazing species have already disappeared, Tobble?" I asked. "How many fantastic creatures, how many wonders, how much wisdom has been lost because of those who have the power to destroy?"

"They make the world a sadder, emptier, uglier place so that they will fit in," Tobble said.

I had never heard him so depressed. I searched for words to cheer him up, but I was too weary with grief myself.

As we rode on through the forest, I tried to imagine it as it must have been before Gaziko's arrival. Had the trees been full of birds? Had deer and poricats frolicked? Had my own people, or Tobble's, once walked these woods picking berries and wildflowers?

Tobble repeated Stump's words:

'Tis ever easier to hate,
Than learn or love, or to create.

"And easier still," I said, "to do nothing to stop evil, to see the horror and look away. To do nothing more than mutter and shake your head."

"We aren't doing nothing," Tobble asked. "Are we?"

"Tobble," I said, managing a wan smile, "we are definitely not doing nothing."

17
The Ragglers

By late afternoon we emerged from Gaziko's cursed forest onto the lowest reaches of the Western Uplands. Two things happened as soon as we felt that balm of pale sunlight on our heads.

First, Havoc picked up the pace, raising his head and moving into the steady trot that had eluded him in the shadows of that awful place.

Second, Tobble and I were instantly hungry.

"I'm starving!" Tobble said.

"So is Havoc." I laughed and pointed to a clear patch of short, browning grass. "He sees his meal."

I let Havoc gallop, and the wind in my fur was a tonic. My eyes streamed from the cold, but the more distance we put between ourselves and the forest, the happier I knew I would be.

When Havoc reached the tasty greens, we climbed down.

Tobble's stomach grumbled mightily, while mine whined.

"It's like our stomachs are talking to each other," Tobble said as he began to unpack food.

"It'll be chilly tonight if we don't find kindling," I said.

"No need to worry. If we ride hard, we'll reach the edge of Lucabena Wood. We'll find plenty there to feed a cheery fire."

I winced. "Another forest?" I asked.

"Oh, no, Byx. It's nothing like that horrible place. You'll see!"

After we'd eaten, we continued our long day's ride across softly rolling hills. I was so saddle sore, I suggested more than once that we just bed down, kindling or no kindling, although the air was quite brisk and a fire would have been most welcome. My legs were numb and my fingers might as well have been sausages, for all the sensation I got from them.

"By now," Tobble said, "I expect that the ragglers have probably spotted us. They have excellent eyesight, you know, almost as keen as raptidons."

"Ragglers?"

"Certainly ragglers." Then, realizing I had no clue what a raggler was, he explained, "They're a wonderful species. They've always been good friends to wobbyks. We trade with them. Some of the fish and oysters we catch, in return for honey and clever woodworking, and of course, they weave the nets we use to catch the fish, so, you see . . ."

Tobble petered out, having lost his train of thought.

We rode on, cold but optimistic, into the setting sun. Darkness fell and thick clouds rolled in. Once again we lacked stars for guidance.

"Don't worry about that," Tobble said. "You'll see."

I didn't have long to wait. Lucabena Wood was no more than a quarter league away. To my surprise, lights, violet and gold, began to twinkle on the horizon like colorful stand-ins for the stars.

As we rode closer still, I caught music drifting on the breeze. I heard no words, just music, a sound like the low-register bowing of a viol.

We rode into trees of great age and no small size, but with none of the overpowering gloom of Gaziko's wretched forest. The trees were well-spaced, leaving plenty of open ground. The lights we'd seen were closer, hopping like large squirrels from branch to branch over our heads. At first I thought they were moving lanterns. But soon I realized that the lights were actually the ragglers themselves, small, spiny creatures emitting a soft glow.

"They shine!" I cried.

"Of course they do," said Tobble. "Why do you think we call them ragglers?"

It made no sense, but I didn't care. After the foulness of Gaziko's forest and the long, cold ride across the uplands, arriving here was like coming home. I felt not just safe, but welcome. It almost seemed I could hear sweet voices in my head, wordless, but understandable—and, most importantly, kind.

"It feels like a welcoming place," I said, watching a raggler move from limb to limb.

"Of course it is." Tobble laughed. "Can't you hear their greetings?"

"Your ears are better than mine, Tobble, but I haven't heard any actual words of welcome."

"Nor will you. Ragglers don't use words. The music you hear is not . . . Here, try something. Cover your ears."

I did. It took a few seconds for me to understand. "I can still hear the music!"

"Yes," Tobble said, pleased. "Ragglers make no sound for ears to hear. They're heard in your mind and in your heart."

"Amazing! I wish I could see one of them more closely."

"Do you?" Tobble said. "Turn around."

There, standing easily on Havoc's haunches, was a creature half the size of Tobble, glowing a soft yellow tinged with violet.

"Ahh!" I cried in surprise.

I heard music then, or rather, a feeling of music, and even without words, I knew what it meant.

Be at peace, friend.

I studied the little creature. Its compact body was covered not in fur or feathers, but in spikes half as long as a human's finger. It was the tips of those spikes that glowed with light. The raggler's legs were squat, its arms long and thin. It had two enormous eyes, not unlike a wobbyk. An additional stalk grew out of the top of its head, and on the end of that was a third eye.

"Greetings, friend raggler," said Tobble. "I am Tobble of the Bossyp wobbyks. This is my friend, Byx of the dairnes."

Not knowing how to greet the tiny creature, I extended my hand.

"No!" Tobble said sharply. "Sorry, Byx, I didn't mean to startle you. But there's a reason why ragglers are so unafraid and welcoming. You see, their skin, and especially their spikes, are poisonous to every species but one: wobbyks. Only the soles of their feet are safe to touch. The ragglers fear no one, and with good reason."

We rode deeper into the woods, drawn by the secret, wordless music that somehow we both understood to mean *Come this way.*

With every minute's ride, the trees grew more festooned with luminous ragglers. Many were sitting in upper branches on fantastic platforms built of a woven material that reminded me of stiff fishermen's nets.

Ragglers were on the ground, too, following us as well as they could on their short legs. Some grabbed hanging vines and were promptly hauled up into the branches. Others slid down trunks to take a closer look at us and offer their welcome.

Half an hour's easy ride brought us to a dense stand of trees so full of the sweet creatures it shone like a tiny, wayward sun.

"I think these are what they call the heart trees," said Tobble. "The center for all ragglers."

"Do they have a king or queen?" I asked.

"Ragglers?" Tobble asked, taken aback by my question. "No, of course not. They rule themselves."

"But how can that be? Who decides what they should do?"

Tobble shrugged. "They do. All ragglers are equal. If it's a matter for the whole species to decide, they commune among themselves, singing their different songs, until a tune emerges and they begin to harmonize. All of it is silent, of course."

"Of course," I said, as if it were obvious.

"I think they want us to stop here," said Tobble.

I craned my neck to gaze at the glowing tree above me. Hundreds of pairs of eyes stared down at us. Hundreds of stalk eyes spiraled in every direction.

"Hello," I said.

Hello, the ragglers sang.

"Would it be all right if we camped here for the night?" Tobble asked.

Of course! they answered. *Please do!*

A simple sentiment, but one so welcome, after all we'd been through, that tears came to my eyes.

18
The Surprise of Kindness

In a land increasingly ruled by the thuggish Murdano, the ragglers' joyful hospitality made me self-conscious about the sword at my side. I removed it and propped my scabbard and shield against a tree.

"May we build a small fire?" I asked.

This took some consideration, apparently. In my head, but not in my ears, I heard a dozen different snatches of tunes. Within seconds, just as Tobble had described, only a few melodies persisted, and then, as if on cue, a single strand of music was left. *You may build a fire*, it went, *but you must be cautious.*

Taking their own advice, a dozen ragglers carrying tiny shovels slid down vines. Working with remarkable speed and efficiency, they dug a shallow pit. Out of the darkness came more ragglers carrying stones, which they set in a ring around the pit.

A stream of dead twigs, sent from the treetops, landed in

the hole. "They've provided kindling," Tobble said. "But they have no fire of their own."

We unpacked Havoc and tied him off. Seeing this, more ragglers arrived, carrying fresh-cut hay and a bucket of water.

I knew Havoc was merely a horse. Nevertheless, I could swear he turned a startled gaze toward me upon witnessing this generosity. Had we all, Havoc included, come to expect nothing from the world but threats and danger? How had that become normal, while kindness seemed strange?

Tobble dug out the tinderbox. I took the flint and steel and struck sparks. Once I had a tiny flame going, Tobble arranged the pieces of kindling into a pyramid. The fire took hold and I said, "Well, that's good, Tobble, but we're going to need larger branches to really—"

I fell silent. Emerging from the woods came three teams of four ragglers each, hauling what to them must have seemed massive—but to me were perfectly sized—logs to add to the fire.

With a hearty blaze going, Tobble and I fell to preparing a simple meal. Just as I was thinking about retrieving our waterskins, I glanced down and realized a row of six tiny cups had appeared on the ground beside me.

"They are the perfect hosts!" I said.

"So long as you come in peace," Tobble said, stirring his pot. "If you'd come to cut down trees? Why then, you'd find yourself under a hailstorm of ragglers. You'd be pierced by poison spikes and die in agony."

I gulped. "Ah. Then we'd better behave ourselves."

After we'd eaten and warmed our toes by the fire, we were joined by a raggler glowing like a splendid sunset. His song asked whether we cared to tell why we were traveling through the Lucabena Wood.

"We are sent by the Lady," I answered, "to ask for help from the wobbyks in stopping a terrible war."

Who is this Lady you speak of?

"She has an army of thousands with her. She means to stop the destruction of homes and farms. And trees," I added hastily. "We wish no more trees to die."

The trees are our mothers.

"I suppose that's true," I agreed. I felt like a madman, carrying on a conversation in which only I spoke.

The air we breathe comes from trees.

It seemed like a quaint notion. Trees making air? But, I supposed, people were free to believe what they wanted.

"My people, the dairnes, often build nests in trees," I said.

The raggler seemed to like that. But then he asked, *Why do you carry a sword and shield?*

I smiled. "Because I have no spikes, my friend."

I was rewarded with a silent song that I somehow knew was a wave of laughter. It was a relief to know the ragglers had a sense of humor.

At first light we will guide you on your way.

"I believe, Tobble, that they have just, in the politest way possible, told us that in the morning we must move on."

"Indeed," Tobble said, nodding his approval. "Very polite and proper."

The glowing spokesman returned to the treetops, raised by vine. Tobble and I laid out our bedrolls, and for the first time in longer than I could remember, I felt secure in the knowledge that, for this one night at least, we were safe.

Warm, fully fed, and with time to think, I lay awake brooding about my friends. I was concerned for all of them, but it was Khara who worried me most. She had such a crushing weight of responsibility on her young shoulders.

In time I drifted into a deep sleep. I dreamed of war and bloodshed and death, and of decency and forgiveness and peace. I dreamed of my first family, the one I would never see again, and of my second family, the one I desperately hoped to see again soon.

When I opened my eyes the next morning, I was startled to see hundreds of ragglers in the tree above me. It was daylight, so they no longer glowed, though they were still tinted in golds and violets. Next to me, Tobble was just waking up.

Tobble blinked at me. "Did you hear what they're singing?"

I frowned. Did I . . . yes. I did. But it seemed absurd. "Are they saying they might help us stop the war?"

Tobble nodded.

"But we never asked them. And anyway, what could they do?"

"We didn't need to ask them. They heard our dreams."

127

"They . . . what, now?" It was an alarming thought. Most of the time I didn't remember my own dreams upon waking. These spiky little creatures were not only seeing them, but discussing them?

"Didn't I tell you? I'm very sorry, how inconsiderate of me. Yes, one of the things that's so interesting about ragglers is the way they can hear thoughts. In fact, they don't hear sounds at all. Just the music of your mind."

I rubbed my eyes. "It's probably better that I didn't know."

I looked up at the treetops. I didn't understand how to send thoughts, so I simply asked, "Friends, how can you help?"

The answer was again wordless and lyrical, pictures that simply unfolded in my brain.

I gasped, grabbing for Tobble's arm.

"Tobble," I whispered.

"Yes, Byx?"

"I think this might be an important thing."

"Very important."

"We'll need to convince your people. And Sabito and Stimball will have to persuade the raptidons. But if those things happen . . ."

I couldn't finish my thought. It was too hopeful, and if I'd learned anything, it was that hope wasn't always enough.

And yet, as we packed up our gear and saddled Havoc, that was all I heard in my head. A tuneless, voiceless song that somehow resolved into a single thought: *There is still hope.*

19
A Wobbyk Reunion

After leaving the ragglers, we'd planned on a three-day ride to Bossyp. But the first snow of the year began to fall, a light dusting at first, soon followed by fat flakes. We ended up spending most of the second day sheltering in an abandoned lean-to.

The crude shack must have belonged to a shepherd, because we found rusted shearing scissors and a stack of burlap bags used to carry fleece to market. We were atop a low hill, not too far from the water's edge. To our great delight, we discovered a small shed, well stocked with firewood and kindling. We made a little fire in the simple hearth and watched half a dozen different types of birds wading along the rocky shore, while eagles circled overhead, using their amazing eyes to spot tasty fish in the shallow waters.

Tobble was obviously excited to be so close to his

homeland. He spent hours telling me about how he'd learned to fish with his father and uncle, and regaled me with stories about his many siblings. How he could keep them all straight was beyond me.

It felt wonderful to see my dear friend full of such anticipation, but in truth, I had a pang of sadness, even jealousy, as I listened to Tobble. I knew it was wrong, and I berated myself for being so small and selfish. But he had a family, a home, a village to return to. And I did not.

Tobble must have sensed my feelings, because that evening he said, "Byx, I wish you could be doing what I'm about to do. If only you could go home, too."

"Thank you, friend." I paused, listening to windblown snow skimming the roof. "But I try to remind myself that at least I'm alive. Unlike . . . everyone else." I reached for his paw. "And truly, Tobble, I am so happy for you."

We fell asleep, huddled side by side. It helped us both stay warm. But I knew, for me at least, that it was comforting to have Tobble's steady snoring so close.

The next morning we shoved open the shed door to find endless sheets of sparkling white. The snow was up to my waist, and head-high for Tobble. We decided to push on, and Havoc managed well enough. But in the afternoon, storm clouds rolled in, and this time the snow was not playing games. It fell all night without pause, and we found ourselves longing for the little shed. We spread blankets over low branches to serve as a roof, then shivered through the night and into a gloomy morning.

"Havoc can't handle this much snow," I said. "We could be stuck here for a few days until the snow melts, but if the weather stays cold, it could be until next spring."

"I certainly hope not!" Tobble exclaimed. "We'll starve. Or freeze. Or starve and then freeze. We're trapped! Stuck!"

He paced back and forth on the narrow patch of muddy ground beneath our "tent."

"I cannot let Khara down," I muttered. "She's counting on us to recruit your people."

"We're so close," Tobble cried. "It's not fair!"

"Look! Ships," I said, pointing, mostly to distract Tobble from his growing panic.

"Ships?" he asked, startled. He shaded his eyes and looked out to sea. "Those aren't ships, just fishing boats. They're low in the water, so they must have a good catch. Soon they'll head for harbor. They could carry us, if only they knew we wished it."

"Too bad they can't hear us," I mused. "I suppose we could wave our hands frantically." I heaved a sigh. Then an idea took hold. "Tobble, did you pack some of the dry kindling from that little shed?"

He understood immediately and unbundled the sticks and grass, while I set to work with steel and flint. It took several tries, but finally we had a fire going.

A small fire that would not last long.

Tobble craned his head back and looked up at the smoke rising from the fire. "More smoke," he said. "The fire's too small, but they might notice smoke. Gather some damp grass from under the snow!"

We both fell to our knees, sticking freezing hands into the snow to yank up fistfuls of grass. It worked. The fire acting on the damp grass made a satisfying pillar of smoke.

To add to our chances, we each grabbed a burning kindling stick and waved it in the air.

"They'll see the smoke, and if they squint hard enough, they'll see us," Tobble said. "They're fishermen. They keep a sharp lookout."

The boat took an hour to draw near, and it came no closer than a quarter league. But to our relief, a longboat was launched from it. And not just any longboat.

"They're two of my brothers!" Tobble cried. "Helloooo, Piddlecombe! Helloooo, Horgle!"

Piddlecombe and Horgle leapt out into the surf, yanked the boat onto the wet sand, and dashed up the snowy embankment toward Tobble. Both wobbyks were taller than Tobble, but they shared my friend's huge ears, long whiskers, and protruding tummy.

The three of them embraced as one, sobbing and laughing and shouting all at once. It made my heart swell to see Tobble's elated smile.

"Wait!" the tallest brother cried. He pointed to Tobble's three carefully braided tails, tied with a leather cord. "You . . . what . . . how?" Dumbstruck, he pointed to his own three loose tails.

The other brother, whose tails were also unbraided, was more direct. "Who gave you permission to braid your tails? And why?"

I couldn't believe it. I knew that the tail-braiding ceremony wobbyks called a "stibillary" was an important rite of passage. Still and all, the brothers hadn't seen Tobble in months. They might well have presumed him dead. Yet his braid was what they focused on?

Tobble puffed out his chest. "I may have performed certain admirable acts."

"Acts of bravery and selflessness," I added.

"As for who gave me permission," Tobble continued, "why, it was the Lady of Nedarra herself, leader of the Army of Peace."

The brothers went speechless, mouths agape. They turned to me for confirmation.

"Yes," I said. "Your brother Tobble is quite important now. In fact, we're here on the Lady's business."

Talking up my faithful friend gave me great pleasure. But not as much pleasure as it gave Tobble himself. I could have sworn he grew an inch taller while I watched.

"Piddlecombe, Horgle, allow me to introduce you to my

dear friend, Byx of the dairnes."

Horgle, the taller of the two, gave a bow, and Piddlecombe followed suit. "A dairne," Piddlecombe marveled. "Well, I'll be."

"And you know the Lady of Nedarra?" Horgle asked. "You've actually met her?"

Tobble tilted his chin. "Indeed, I count myself as both her loyal servant and her friend."

"We thought you were . . . you know," said Piddlecombe. "A goner."

"He's come close." I patted Tobble on the back. "But your brother, as I'm sure you know, is a fierce warrior when he needs to be."

The brothers gave nervous nods. Tobble was practically floating on air, he was so enjoying the moment.

"If you would be so kind, Brothers," he said. "As you heard, we're on a mission of the greatest importance, a matter of life and death. Take us to Bossyp at once!"

He was clearly enjoying his new authority, but being a wobbyk, he had to add, "If it's not too much trouble."

20
Making an Entrance

The wind was against us through that night, so we crowded together. The sound of Tobble and his brothers, snoring in near-unison, was soothing music to my weary ears. In the morning we boarded the longboat and returned to the off-shore fishing vessel. It was a cramped and unsettling, if brief, trip for Havoc, but he'd grown used to being unsettled. He clambered up a ramp with ease, and soon an offshore breeze filled the fishing boat's sail and we skimmed away.

The land reeled by, mostly fallow pastures dotted with stands of snow-blanketed trees. It looked like gentle, pleas-ant country. A countryside kept gentle and pleasant, at least in part, because the ragglers blocked much of the land route.

Tobble had tried to describe a wobbyk village to me, but as we tacked northwest and his little town came into view,

I realized he hadn't begun to do it justice. It was like something out of a child's dream.

Wobbyks live underground for the most part, so I knew that the village was crisscrossed by a vast network of tunnels. What I hadn't realized was that wobbyks also build aboveground huts in the shape of cones. From the centers of most cones rose a tree, sometimes a thin birch sapling, sometimes a massive oak. The bigger the tree, the taller the cone hut. Some of the huts were easily six times my own height.

Each hut was painted in one of six bright colors: purple, gold, turquoise, spring green, pink, or ocean blue. Bossyp extended up the side of a small slope, revealing patterns in the hut colors: a streak of purple, a circle of gold, a jagged lightning bolt of pink. Each color was distinct, occupying a specific area, a bit like a neighborhood in a city.

"It's delightful!" I exclaimed. "When you said wobbyks built tunnels, you never mentioned all the rest of this."

Tobble frowned. "Didn't I? Surely you didn't think we lived like moles or rabbits. You can't very well have a proper tunnel without a hut to shield the opening from rain and snow."

"True enough. But what about the trees?"

"Well, Byx, we don't want rain pouring in, but we do want water. So when it rains—and mind you, it rains frequently in Bossyp—water runs down the bark in little streams. It collects in underground pools, then funnels into channels that we use for drinking and washing. My goodness, we wouldn't want a tunnel without running water!"

"I suppose not," I allowed, though running water was almost unheard of, even in great cities or the Murdano's palace. "And the wonderful colors?"

"Oh, that. Each family has its own color. There are six families, six colors."

"And how many wobbyks in a family?"

He shrugged. "I have five hundred direct relatives, and another thousand or so who are relatives by marriage or adoption. We're a small family. The turquoise is us. The pinks have ten thousand members, the purples, twice that number. In all, we number the population of Bossyp at sixty-one thousand. At least, that's what it was when I was last here."

Our boat had to pass Bossyp, turn due north, and then veer east in order to come around to the north side of the village. The harbor was filled with dozens of wobbyk boats in many shapes and sizes, either moored with anchors or drawn up onto the small beach.

We docked at a long, low pier with scarcely a bump. "There's a crowd waiting for us," I said.

"Certainly there's a crowd. It would be terribly impolite if no one was there to greet us."

"I suppose it would."

"Come, Byx, let me show you off," said Tobble. "I mean, show you around."

He led the way across a short gangplank to the pier. It was a relief to step foot back on dry land, as I'd been feeling a bit seasick. But it was odd, too. For one thing, while I was small and insignificant in a human village, I was a giant in Bossyp. Tiny wobbyk kits, no bigger than puppies, shyly touched my fur.

"Well, hello," I said. The kits giggled. One of them tossed me a little ball made of woven reeds, and I lobbed it back.

An older wobbyk came running up and shooed the kits away. "Don't bother our important guest!"

I began to say that I wasn't at all bothered—in fact, the kits had reminded me how long it had been since I'd been playful—but I was interrupted by a joyous shout from Tobble. He was in the tight embrace of two elderly wobbyks, a male and a female, both of whom were sobbing.

"My baby," cried the female, her gray-tipped ears trembling. "My teeny-tiny Tobble the Terrible."

She glanced at me through shining eyes. "This little guy had quite a temper as a kit."

"He still does," I said with a laugh.

Tobble managed to extricate himself from their paws. "Mibs and Pobs," he said, "allow me to introduce you to my dearest friend in the whole wide world, Byx of the dairnes. I mean Ambassador Byx." He grinned. "Byx, these are my parents, Ollywink and Rosegirdle."

"But you must call us Mibs and Pobs!" exclaimed Olly-wink, and instantly I was wrapped in the arms of Tobble's father and mother.

I wiped away tears. It had been so long since I'd been hugged by my own parents. I'd forgotten how sweet and comforting it felt to be held.

"Your tails, my son!" Ollywink exclaimed, pointing to Tobble's braid.

"I've much to tell you both," said Tobble, "but first, I have work to do." He nodded at me. "Ambassador Byx," he said with sudden, stiff formality, "I would take you to the bileraka."

"The what?"

"The bileraka, is our, um . . ." Tobble scrunched up his face, trying to find the right word. "You know how there's a Murdano and a Kazar and mayors and village elders and all that sort of thing?" He waved a hand. "Important people who make decisions and such."

"I see," I said uncertainly.

"We have six elders in the bileraka," said Ollywink. "And our newest member is none other than your very own mibs, Tobble!"

"Mibs! I'm so proud of you!" Tobble exclaimed, and she beamed at his praise.

"She won by a landslide," Ollywink added. He winked at

Tobble. "Seems I have two influential family members these days."

With Ollywink and Rosegirdle on either side of me, I followed Tobble, who strutted quite boldly through the crowd. We came to one of the larger cones surrounding a thick-limbed evergreen. The cone featured a low door, high enough for a wobbyk to walk through, but so small that I had to drop to all fours.

Once inside, I discovered that the cone covered a hole. The tree grew up in the center, but with space all around. The sides of the hole had been chiseled into winding stairs, but the steps were awfully narrow for my big feet.

"Come, there's another way," said Tobble, after I nearly slid down the steps on my tail. He raised his voice. "A line! A line for Ambassador Byx!"

As if by magic, a vine curled down from within the tree branches. With a wink at Tobble, I said, "I have another idea."

The hole went straight down for perhaps thirty feet, with the tree trunk in the center. That left me enough room.

I spread my arms and extended my glissaires. With easy grace, I tipped forward and glided around and around the tree, descending slowly as warm air from below gave me lift.

It was a silly thing to do, perhaps. But fun, too. I'd almost forgotten what fun was like.

I landed on all fours and stood, only to find that I'd dropped onto a sort of platform shaped like a semicircle around the roots of the great tree. I was in an underground amphitheater.

Around me, to my embarrassment, at least a hundred wobbyks stood patiently, although a handful were seated at the front on a wooden bench. The entire group appeared to be awaiting my arrival, although I was pretty sure they hadn't expected me to glide in. It was a childish stunt, I supposed, and not the way ambassadors were meant to arrive.

Tobble slid down a vine and landed beside me. "Well, that was unexpected," he whispered.

"Sorry. I just..." But I had no good explanation. I'd wanted for a minute not to be thinking life and death, war and peace. I didn't want to be Ambassador Byx; I wanted to just be me.

But of course, that wasn't possible. I had work to do.

21
Truth and Lies

Tobble held up his paws and the crowd instantly fell silent.

"Members of the bileraka," he began, nodding as Rose-girdle took her seat with the five other elders. "My family, my fellow wobbyks of all families, welcome. I present to you the ambassador for the Lady of Nedarra, Byx of the dairnes."

I suspected that the few wobbyks who weren't already surprised by my strange arrival were definitely shocked by that last word: dairne.

"A dairne?" someone yelped, quickly adding, "I apologize for my outburst."

"There are no dairnes!" someone else cried. "They were declared extinct. Of course, I mean no offense."

A graying wobbyk, one of the bileraka members, pointed a walking stick at me. "Put him to the test! If that's not too great an imposition."

It wasn't exactly how I'd hoped to begin this extremely important meeting.

"Please, my brothers and sisters," Tobble pleaded. "Show respect for the Lady's ambassador."

More wobbyks were arriving via three tunnels, while still others slid down vines or skittered down the stairs. Kits sat on the shoulders of their parents. Every available space seemed to be filled with curious wobbyks. The air was warm and damp, and I felt a bit light-headed.

"Some lady, some dairne," came a voice loaded with doubt. "We must have proof. If the alleged dairne is not too offended by the suggestion."

I was being heckled by wobbyks. Heckled very politely. But still heckled.

Quickly I reminded myself that I had a job to do, and an important one, at that. Before I could ask for help from these wobbyks, I would need to earn their trust.

I held up a hand. "I'm not offended in the least. Of course you have every right to ask for proof. What proof might I offer?"

The louder wobbyks had formed a group at the front. "Truth and lies!" one of them called out.

"Of course," I said, nodding, doing my best to seem reasonable and mature. "Perhaps several of you could make statements. I'll tell you whether or not you speak the truth."

Clearly this was agreeable to the audience, as several

applauded politely.

"I am Halfibble," a stout wobbyk said.

"Hello, Halfibble," I said. "And I don't wish to offend, but that is not your true name."

My words were met with a wave of delighted laughter. I'd performed a trick, and the audience liked it.

"Halfibble" bowed to me and said, "You are correct. My name is Vintiggle. I am pleased to meet you."

"Likewise, friend wobbyk," I said, returning the bow.

"I am Murdaddle," a female wobbyk said. "This morning I took milk from my six sheplets. In all it was four gallons."

"I am very sorry to contradict you, friend wobbyk, but you do not have six sheplets. And you did not draw four gallons of milk."

Murdaddle cocked her head. "Then what is the correct number?"

"That I cannot say. I can only say whether a statement is true or false. And to be more specific, I can only tell whether you *believe* it to be true or false."

I'd performed much the same routine before the Murdano himself. That had been terrifying. This was somewhere between amusing and worrying. After all, I'd come here on a mission, not to provide free entertainment to the Bossyp community.

"I am called Elder Diggle. I will say five things." This

announcement came from a bileraka member, a wobbyk so old that his ears drooped low and his green eyes were clouded. "If you correctly identify the true and the false of all five, you will have proven yourself to be a dairne."

"I await your five statements, Elder Diggle."

"One: I am two hundred and nine years old."

"False."

"Two: I have three hundred and twenty-nine grandchildren."

"Then congratulations, sir, for that is both true and impressive."

"Three: I prefer mead to wine."

This earned a laugh, which rather gave away the truth, but I played along. "Friend Diggle, I believe that to be false."

"Four," he said, undeterred. "I once hauled in a fish three times my own size."

"Goodness," I said. "You must have had food for weeks."

"Well, we had to dry a great deal of it. Salted and dried. But the fresh steaks were—" He stopped himself, realizing he'd lost track of his goal. "And the fifth and final statement."

"I am prepared," I said.

"Five: I am responsible for the deaths twenty years ago of six members of my family. Due to a careless misreading of a storm, which ended by capsizing our boat."

I didn't need dairne powers to know he believed it. His

voice quavered. This was a tale he had told many times before. It was the guilt that had shadowed his life ever since.

It was an unsettling moment. I forgot that I was trying to prove myself a dairne. I just saw the wobbyk's guilt, so like my own.

I hopped down off the low platform and went to him, taking his hand in mine. "My friend, I know that you believe that. And I understand it, for I too carry a terrible guilt in my heart. The death of my entire family, my people. I was off playing. I wasn't there when the soldiers of the Murdano butchered everyone I loved."

His huge round eyes filled with tears, and so did mine. For long seconds it was just the two of us, the ancient wobbyk and the too-young dairne, united by guilt.

I looked up and saw that every wobbyk in the room was watching. No one made a sound.

"But I can also see in the eyes of your fellow wobbyks that they don't blame you, Elder Diggle. I don't need special dairne powers to feel the great respect and affection these wobbyks have for you. So I say this: You spoke the truth as you believe it. But you didn't speak the truth."

Elder Diggle smiled wistfully. "And you, friend dairne— for you are most certainly a dairne—do you still carry the guilt despite what anyone else says?"

I met his gaze. Words were impossible. I could only nod.

"Ah," said Elder Diggle. He patted my back and looked

over at Tobble. "You travel in good company, Tobble."

"I do," Tobble said proudly.

With that, Elder Diggle dismissed most of the crowd. "Come now, you've had your entertainment. Back to work! Are there no nets to mend? Are there no hulls to scrape?"

The wobbyks filed away obediently, though many clearly wished to stay. In the end, Tobble and I found ourselves standing with the six elders: Diggle, Shaffleton, Swoopert, Gullbabble, Tillimud, and Rosegirdle.

Elder Swoopert, an older female, led us through a tight tunnel to a small offshoot room. It was charming and colorful, if tiny.

"Please," said Elder Swoopert. "Have a seat. We have much to discuss."

The eight of us sat down. We would tell our stories. They would hear my pleas. And perhaps—just perhaps—we would decide the fate of the world.

22
Dark News

That night, the wobbyks provided us with a lovely hut reserved for distinguished visitors. My bed was a cushioned platform suspended by blue vines dotted with tiny, fragrant white flowers shaped like butterflies. A crackling blaze in a nearby hearth meant that I could turn to one side and then the other, warming myself pleasantly. Tobble had a matching bed on the other side of the fire. Although our hammocks were underground, a wide opening far above us revealed a circle of silver stars.

I was deeply weary. Our talk with the elders had gone on for hours, through two delicious meals and a post-dinner toast. After that, Tobble had insisted on introducing me to many, many, many of his relatives.

Many.

I expected to fall asleep instantly, but the sky was so clear, the stars so bright, that I lay awake for hours. Early the next morning, having finally allowed sleep to overtake me, I was awakened by frantic shrieking coming from every direction, it seemed.

"Peril! Peril! Wobbyks arise! Peril!"

I tumbled out of my hammock. Tobble was already awake and quivering.

"What is it?" I asked.

"We're under attack!"

"What? Who? Who is attacking us?"

He pointed skyward. There, floating in the early morning air, was a raptidon.

"Wait," I said, grabbing Tobble by the arm. "Didn't we see that hawk with Rorid Headcrusher?"

Rorid Headcrusher lived far away to the southeast in a large rookery. He was a terrifying old bird, but he'd provided us with help early in our journey, and I knew him to be fair and honest. In fact, he was the one who'd sent Stimball to our war council.

"I think you're right," said Tobble.

"We need to get to the surface," I said.

"Climb the vine or take the stairs?" Tobble said. "Your choice. Or I can call for someone to haul you up."

"Stairs," I said. Stumbling repeatedly over my too-large feet, I slowly made my way up the narrow staircase. Tobble followed behind me.

Once outside our hut, we were buffeted by a rush of wobbyks racing past. I could see just how prepared they were for raptidon trouble. Two hundred archers, arrows nocked, awaited orders.

"Please! Don't attack!" I cried. "At least not yet."

The wobbyk in charge made a hand motion, and the archers stood down, to my relief.

"Hey, up there!" I called. "Have you come from Lord Rorid?"

The circling hawk stared down at me with pitiless black-and-yellow eyes. I could well understand the wobbyks' terror. Raptidons have no trouble carrying off creatures the size of wobbyks.

"Aye," the raptidon replied. "I am Dothram. I have a message from Lord Rorid and the Lady."

The hawk circled down to land atop a hay cart. He had a sharply curved beak, red-and-orange wings, and a shimmering black tail.

"You were one of Rorid Headcrusher's guards, I believe," I said. "It's good to see you again." I very nearly tried to shake his "hand," but you don't grab a raptidon's talons any more than you'd grab the wrong end of a knife.

"I am delighted to find you still alive, Ambassador Byx."

"And I am delighted to still be alive."

I think he laughed. Raptidon laughter is almost as unsettling as felivet laughter.

"I come with foul news," said Dothram. "Woad's men have gone up into the Perricci Mountains. Their plan was to block a Dreylander breakout once the terramants complete their tunnel. But the Kazar has been clever. He sent a force, small but powerful, through the border passes."

"So the war's started?" Tobble asked, wringing his paws.

"Not yet," said Dothram. "The Lady hopes that we can delay this thrust. Perhaps even stop it altogether with the help of the wobbyks. Have you discussed it with them?"

I winced. Despite our long hours of conversation the previous night, the wobbyk elders hadn't yet come to a decision. They seemed to like Tobble's idea of enlisting the ragglers to help. But they still weren't sure whether to embark on such a dangerous mission.

Elder Diggle approached us, eyeing Dothram warily. "Is there news?"

"None of it good," I said. "The Kazar has sent a small force through the border passes."

"The Lady," said Dothram, "hopes that your people will join mine to deliver a bloody nose to the Dreylanders."

"Does she indeed?" said Diggle. "And what does the Lady offer in return?"

He almost sounded as if he were asking for a bribe. "Are you demanding payment to aid us in stopping a war?" Dothram asked.

"You want us to send our people into battle," Diggle

replied. "A battle in which many wobbyks could perish."

The hawk's gaze softened—as much as that was possible, at any rate. "I meant no disrespect."

Diggle turned to me. "We want nothing but representation for our kind. Though we speak and build, though we farm and fish, we wobbyks are always second-class citizens. We're excluded because we're not one of the governing species. We would like to see that change."

"I have no power to grant such a thing," said Dothram.

Diggle nodded. "Then I ask you, Ambassador Byx, on your honor as a dairne. If we help, and if, when all is done, the Lady has the power to grant it, will you make our case to her?"

"Will I ask the Lady to make wobbyks a governing species?"

"Yes, will you do everything that you can?"

"With all my heart," I said. "I've spent many months with Tobble. If his people, your people, don't deserve a place of respect, then no species does."

Diggle glanced at a group of wobbyks behind him. No words were spoken, but just the same, I could see that they'd reached a verdict.

When he turned back to me, he looked ten years younger. His kindly, wrinkled wobbyk face was suddenly fierce and determined.

"Where, then, do you wish the wobbyks to assemble?" asked Diggle. "There's no time to waste. On that we all agree."

23
Waiting for the Raptidons

Time was precious now.

I fretted as the wobbyks spent half a day selecting their fighters. I fretted as they spent the rest of the day preparing to travel. I fretted as we spent two days more getting from Bossyp back to the nearest edge of the Lucabena Wood.

But once we were camped there at last, 609 wobbyks and one dairne, I relaxed a bit. Dothram was finally ready to fly off and summon his fellows.

"I shall be back in the morning," Dothram said. "If I do not return, you must assume that I have been killed, or that Rorid's authority has been usurped."

"Farewell," I said, "and hurry."

"I will fly as fast as the wind allows," Dothram vowed. "Look for me in the morning!"

With that, he spread his wings and soared away into the

sky, his plumage catching the salmon rays of the setting sun.

Tobble had headed off with some of the elders to speak with the ragglers. He was so puffed up to be part of the delegation that I worried he might explode. Still, it was wonderful to see him feeling such pride.

I spent the evening alone, but not lonely. Sitting at the edge of a hearty bonfire, I listened to wobbyk songs, wobbyk poems, and wobbyk stories of great wobbyks in wobbyk history. By the time I finally headed to my bedroll, I felt I could write a history of the species.

Perhaps all those wobbyk tales were the reason I dreamed that night of Urman's yew, the place where humans, raptidons, felivets, natites, terramants, and dairnes had assembled to find a way to live together. It was there that the six great governing species had agreed to split the world into pieces. It had always seemed a wise and wonderful thing, that treaty. But was it, really? Couldn't they have found a way for all species to live side by side? Instead, the terramants had gone their way, and the felivets theirs, while the humans had built governments that had turned into tyrannies.

Humans, most especially, seemed to have a need to see themselves as alone in the world. Being isolated from other species made it easy for them to hold others in contempt, to destroy my people, to hem in the felivets, even to try to dominate all of nature.

As far as wobbyks went, though, we dairnes weren't free

of guilt. My ancestors had never spoken up for their species. As long as anyone could remember, wobbyks had been ignored—and often worse than ignored.

I wondered if that would ever change. Khara would do what she could, but her goal wasn't to rule. She simply wanted to stop the approaching war and end the destruction of nonhuman species. The Lady of Nedarra was no more interested in being a queen or an empress than I was in being an ambassador.

I woke with the sun, jumped up, and anxiously searched the low-hanging clouds for raptidons. But aside from a single gull, I saw nothing on the wing.

I'd heard Tobble return late in the night. He groaned in the bedroll near mine.

"Have they come?" he asked, yawning and stretching.

"Not yet. But they will. How was your meeting with the ragglers?"

"Very good, I think." He grinned. "I did most of the talking."

"Did you indeed?"

He shrugged. "I did. The elders spoke, too, of course. But when it comes to the wider world and the workings of all the forces, well, I am more knowledgeable."

"My goodness," I teased, "the elders must be very ignorant to defer to you."

"What? But . . . oh, I see, you're making fun of me."

"Only gently and with love."

Tobble laughed. "Well, we have come a long way, you and I. A very long way from being a drowning wobbyk and a desperate endling."

"I sometimes feel as if I've aged twenty years," I admitted.

"When it's all over, we can go back to just being Tobble and Byx."

"Can we?" I asked.

"Of course we can!"

I nodded, but I wondered if Tobble was right. Could we really go back? Once your mind was filled with new knowledge, especially if some of it was heartbreaking, could you ever return to an earlier time?

Elder Diggle and some of his fellow wobbyks appeared while Tobble and I sipped hot tea near the main campfire. "Good morning, Ambassador Byx and Honorable Tobble. Did you sleep well?"

"We did, and thank you," said Tobble. "Will you join us for a cup of tea?"

"Thank you, no, we've all had our tea." With the necessary politeness out of the way, Diggle got down to business. "So," he said, "I do not see a sky filled with friendly raptidons."

"No," I agreed. "Not yet."

"They may have decided it was safer to stay out of the fight."

"Maybe, Elder Diggle, your concerns are reasonable." I hardened my voice. Diggle needed to understand that it was not time to despair. "However, I've met Lord Rorid, and I can assure you that he is not easily frightened or discouraged."

That soothed Diggle. For an hour. Then two hours. But as the morning wore on, even I was having doubts. Had Dothram been killed?

Had the raptidons decided not to fight alongside us? Had they done some kind of dirty deal behind our backs?

Had we been betrayed?

I feared that this, my second mission, would fail. That I would have accomplished nothing. Although I knew it was ridiculous, I think I was more afraid of disappointing Khara than of heading into battle.

I gazed out across the wobbyk encampment. What I saw wasn't encouraging. Some faces were turned to the sky, searching for raptidons. Others were looking at me and scowling.

I turned to see Diggle approaching me yet again. "Ambassador Byx!" he said sharply. "I don't wish to trouble you, but once again I must say: it appears we have all wasted our time!"

"Elder Diggle, as you know, things are very unsettled. I beg you to please allow a few more hours—"

I stopped talking when Tobble clutched my arm. "What is it?" I asked.

Tobble just grinned and pointed. A strange, fast-moving

dark cloud was scudding across the sky.

All across the camp, wobbyks began to point. It was a stirring sight. The small cloud grew larger, as high-flying raptidons dropped down through the overcast sky to join their lower-flying fellows. Hundreds upon hundreds of raptidons appeared: falcons, hawks, turries, ospreys, owls, nutchens, and eagles.

"I believe, Elder Diggle," I said, heaving a relieved sigh, "that our transportation has arrived."

I expected to see Dothram leading the formation. But at their head, surrounded by a half dozen vicious-looking purple hawks, was none other than Rorid Headcrusher himself.

I'd never seen him in the air with his wings spread. He was breathtakingly large, his wingspan double the length of a tall human. Floating down in a spiral, he landed atop a sapling that bowed under his weight. Tobble, Diggle, and I rushed over.

"Lord Rorid," I said, bowing low.

"Byx of the dairnes," Rorid said in his strangled, harsh voice.

"Allow me to present Elder Diggle of the Bossyp wobbyks," I said.

Diggle bowed. Rorid was not the wobbyks' ruler, but he had a certain majesty about him that made bowing seem like the most appropriate reaction.

"Elder Diggle," Rorid said after the unavoidable wobbyk

welcomes and thank-yous and compliments. "Are your people prepared? We fly directly into battle. And it will be night before we arrive."

"The wobbyks of Bossyp are ready," Diggle said solemnly.

I let out a slow breath. I'd accomplished, once again, what Khara had asked of me.

No one cheered. No one spoke of victories to come. The wobbyks didn't want to go into battle any more than I did. But as I'd told Maxyn, courage is not the absence of fear.

We were all afraid.

We just weren't going to let fear stop us.

PART THREE
HEART

24
In Flight

Because I'm a dairne and I have glissaires, I've done my share of gliding through the air. You could call it soaring, as long as you understand that our version of soaring is basically just falling more slowly than most creatures would.

In any case, I've soared.

I soared as a pup, playing with my siblings.

I soared when I rescued Tobble from drowning.

I soared when I nearly ran into Araktik, the Murdano's Seer.

Once upon a time, I might have said that soaring with my glissaires was more or less just like flying.

I might have said that. But now I know better.

Clutched in Rorid's fantastically powerful talons, I dangled from his grip as we passed through the clouds. And Rorid was *flying*.

It was nothing like soaring.

Taking off had been a bit challenging. First Rorid had rested atop a quickly constructed perch. (The wobbyks had built dozens of such perches in mere minutes.) I stood, back to Rorid, and he reached carefully forward, wrapping his talons around first my right shoulder and then my left. Each of his "toes" was as thick as a man's wrist. And each ended in a hooked nail that looked capable of disemboweling a . . . well, a dairne, for one thing.

Rorid's talons clamped under my armpit and over my shoulder. I'd just begun adjusting to that disturbing reality when I heard his wings whip open. I felt a sudden gust of wind as my body lost touch with the earth.

As Rorid beat his wings, I watched my feet float over the snowy fields below. We gained just enough altitude to barely clear the highest trees in the Lucabena Wood. One was so close the topmost leaves tickled my toes.

When a stiff breeze came out of the west, Rorid shot up with ease. I twisted my neck as well as I could and saw hundreds of great raptidons soaring behind us, each with a wobbyk in its talons.

And in the paws of each wobbyk was a raggler.

The wobbyks chattered excitedly, and so did the ragglers in their own way, singing a joyous song. Did they know we were going into battle? Of course. But their song wasn't about that. It was about the singular thrill of being airborne.

We earthbound creatures had been lifted up into the realm of the raptidons. Behind us, the sun plummeted toward the horizon, sending beams of yellow and orange light to glaze feather and fur with gold. It was exhilarating. It was not, however, particularly comfortable. I was hanging by my armpits, my legs dangling awkwardly.

I noticed Tobble, carried by Dothram, approaching on my left side.

"How are you doing, Tobble?" I shouted.

"I'm not afraid, that's for sure," Tobble yelled back, sounding afraid. "It's just that it's a long way down, in case you hadn't noticed."

It occurred to me that I should probably be much more afraid than I was. But Rorid was mighty. He'd ruled a long time and had lived even longer. I trusted him.

Besides, I had no choice but to trust him.

"Listen to the ragglers," I advised Tobble. "They're not concerned."

"Of course they aren't afraid. They're ragglers! If they're dropped, they'll probably just bounce!"

Tobble, like all the other wobbyks, cradled a raggler in his paws. The little creatures weren't heavy, but it was still probably a strain.

The air was frigid, the wind strong. I wondered if the raptidons understood that we ground creatures had limits on how much cold we could stand. On we flew as the sky turned a darker shade of blue, and the ragglers sang their silent but compelling song. My muscles started to cramp, but when the stars appeared, I completely forgot my discomfort.

They seemed so impossibly close! If Rorid flew just a little higher, I felt I could snag one and stick it in my pouch.

"Lord Rorid, may I ask a question?"

"So long as it is one question, perhaps two. But no more. Flying is best done in silence."

"I was just wondering if you worried about running into storm clouds. Or even stars."

"Eh?" Rorid was astonished. "Run into . . . ? Oh, I forget how weak are the eyes of the ground-bound. To answer, we often fly through storms. Rain clouds are quite low, generally. Other clouds can be far beyond the reach of even my wings."

"And the stars?"

"My, my, young dairne, when we are done with all this madness, you really must see to your education! The scholars tell us that the stars are light shining through holes in the great black bowl that covers the earth at night. And that black bowl is many times higher than the highest cloud."

I couldn't look upward to see stars. Staring above me, I saw only Rorid's wings and body, his cruel beak pointing the way. To view the stars, I had to look off to the sides or straight in front of me. But now, looking ahead, I saw a flat, starless black.

"I don't wish to chatter on, Lord Rorid, but why are there no stars ahead?"

"Their light is blocked by clouds. Clouds heavy with snow."

"Snow?"

"Yes. And we have no time to roost and wait for it to pass."

"We're going to fly through a snowstorm?" I asked in alarm.

As if in answer, a lone snowflake landed on my nose.

That single flake seemed rather charming to me. What came next was not at all charming.

Rorid screeched a long string of what sounded like words, although they weren't in the Common Tongue. Orders to his subjects, I decided. Although I didn't understand his language, I did understand his tone. And I understood, too, that the ragglers' song had become much less animated and upbeat.

"This will be difficult for you, Ambassador Byx," Rorid warned me. "We must try to climb above the storm."

Above? Above a storm?

The snow was already much thicker. Mostly it melted on my fur, but little by little a crust of ice formed.

I turned to check on Tobble, but a massive flash burned my eyes, and a second later, my ears nearly burst at the sound of a catastrophically loud boom.

Lightning. Thunder.

I'd been frightened by storms, even in the safety of sturdy shelter on the ground. But flying through the middle of one was quite another thing. I quickly learned to cover my ears the instant I saw a bolt of lightning, as it was always followed by terrifying explosions of thunder that seemed to rattle the very bones within me.

Rorid's wings swept the air back, beat after relentless beat. Ice attached to the trailing edge of his feathers. I could tell by his labored breathing that he was straining. Perhaps we were rising, but I couldn't be sure.

I happened to be glancing toward Tobble when I saw a massive, jagged shaft of lightning strike a raptidon and its wobbyk and raggler passengers.

The raptidon burst into a ball of flame. I cried out in horror as I watched the inferno tumble from the sky.

A dead raptidon. A dead wobbyk. A dead raggler.

I feared they wouldn't be the last.

25
The Dreylanders

The terror of that desperate flight to get above the clouds will be with me always.

Lightning stabbed at us. Thunder shook us. Snow blinded us. My hands and feet were numb. My shoulders ached. Each breath took effort, and soon I was panting just to fill my lungs.

Over and over again the lightning came. It was as if the sky itself had decided to destroy us. Two more raptidons spiraled down in flames as lightning made short-lived fireballs of them.

A few other raptidons, too exhausted to go on, had to seek shelter on the ground with their passengers.

Just as I was ready to beg Rorid to land as well, a miracle occurred: we broke through the clouds. In an instant, we'd moved from despair to a place of silent wonder.

The clouds were below us, spread out like an endless,

lumpy quilt. I could still see lightning, but it had faded to harmless flashes beneath my hanging feet. The stars were so clear and bright I had to blink.

And there was Tobble, just to our left. He'd survived.

"How fare you, Ambassador Byx?" Rorid asked. It was the first thing he'd said in hours.

"Lord Rorid, I am wet down to my bones, so cold I can no longer feel my feet, and my shoulders ache as if I'd been run over by a stampede of garilans. But it's worth it, just to see this."

"It is beautiful," Rorid said, and his raptidon croak almost sounded sweet.

"Still, I grieve for those we lost," I said.

"We knew," said Rorid simply, "this would not be easy."

The air was no warmer, but at least it was drier, and the thunder had retreated into mild grumbling. Rorid flew on, and I suppose it showed just how exhausted I was that I actually fell asleep. From time to time, I'd wake to the reassuring sight of Rorid's mighty wings above me. But I was asleep when he spoke next.

"Wake up, friend dairne," he said. "We are almost there. And there is something you may wish to see."

I opened my eyes and cried out in delight. The sun! Orange and yellow and fierce, it seemed to be lounging on a cushion of clouds.

"Thank you, Lord Rorid. I'm very glad to wake to a sight

like this." After a moment to orient myself, I said, "The sun's on our right. We've turned north?"

"Yes. We follow the river Telarno. My falcon scouts have flown low. They encountered sparrows and gulls who gave them news of a battle that took place during the night. Woad's brave humans were ambushed by an enemy force. They've suffered terrible losses. Now the Dreylanders are camped just outside a village called Broog." Rorid paused. "Soon they'll fall upon Broog and massacre every living creature, then burn the village to ashes."

I absorbed his words like blows. *Terrible losses. Massacre. Burn.* An image, unbidden, came to me of the moment I'd first laid eyes on the dead bodies of my family and friends after the Murdano's soldiers had wreaked their havoc.

I clenched my fists and willed away the picture in my head.

Dothram veered in close to Rorid, almost wing tip to wing tip.

"Tobble!" I called. "Are you all right?"

"Of course. Why shouldn't I be?" He seemed genuinely puzzled.

"You're not half-frozen and aching in every muscle?"

He laughed. "Byx, my friend, you're much bigger than I am. The weight of your own body must strain your joints. Also, my raggler sang to me all night," he added. "It was most comforting."

I wondered if Tobble had witnessed the fiery deaths I'd seen. Perhaps somehow he'd missed them. I considered sharing Rorid's news about the Dreylanders. But Tobble seemed so content. He'd know soon enough, in any case.

Rorid, speaking Raptidon, gave instructions to Dothram, who swerved off. Tobble held his raggler with one paw and waved to me with the other.

"Now, Ambassador Byx," said Rorid, "we must find a place to set you down safely."

"Set me down? We're not going to stop the Dreylanders?"

"Battle is no place for an ambassador," Rorid replied. "You are important to the Lady. I would not wish to have to report your death."

I hesitated. Rorid made sense. Almost. I was of very little use in battle. And the prospect terrified me. I'd seen enough to imagine the worst.

I was an ambassador. Wasn't I? My duty was to Khara, wasn't it?

But Tobble was going. How could I not?

"No, Lord Rorid. I have to be with my wobbyk friends. They're here because of me."

I think Rorid chuckled. It's hard to tell with raptidons. "As you wish, Ambassador Byx. Draw your weapon. It is time."

Rorid changed the beat of his wings slightly, and soon we were surrounded by hundreds of raptidons, each armed with a wobbyk and a raggler.

I rubbed my hands together to get some blood back in them. After adjusting the strap on the shield Varis had given me, I drew my sword.

Rorid issued a deafening cry. All across the sky, raptidons spilled air from their wings, shooting like falling arrows down into the clouds. Down into wet cotton. Down into half-blindness.

Faster and faster we moved, until I could barely keep my eyes open against the wind.

I glimpsed a wisp-obscured hint of land.

In seconds we were directly above the village of Broog. It looked to be a simple place, just thatched cottages and crooked streets dusted with snow, all surrounded by a crude palisade. Inside the village, I saw mothers, children, and a few older people, all humans as far as I could tell, clearing the streets and dashing into houses.

Near the palisade gate stood a cluster of men and women. They weren't soldiers, clearly. Here and there I saw swords, but most carried pitchforks, hoes, and sticks sharpened to points that couldn't penetrate the thinnest leather jerkin.

Outside the gate were Woad's people, what was left of them. Perhaps a hundred were there, many bandaged and hobbling, others lying on stretchers.

Woad had formed his warriors into a shield wall, each shield held to overlap the ones on either side. Behind the wall, a dozen big men, spears raised, stood ready to plug any gap.

It was professional and impressive. No one but a fool would want to attack that grim barrier.

Except for one heart-wrenching fact. The shield wall was made up of fifty humans, from end to end.

Approaching them were a thousand warriors in the livery of the Kazar. Each was well armed. Each seemed fresh and eager. At best, Woad's fighters could only look determined, if weary.

The Dreylanders also had a shield wall. It was four times the length of Woad's. Row upon row of warriors stood ready to replace the front line. For the most part, they were humans, but I saw a half-dozen felivets roaming the ends of the shield wall, and four great terramants with human warriors riding atop their shiny, segmented backs.

Behind the line of horse-size insects stood a man dressed more finely than the rest, armor glittering.

"Their general," I muttered.

"Indeed," Rorid said. "And he is mine!"

26
The First Battle

The raptidons veered as one to the east, past the battlefield below. "When you attack from the air," Rorid explained, "it is good to have the light at your back. Ground dwellers are blinded by the sun."

We flew on, unnoticed, it seemed, by the Dreylanders or Woad's soldiers. As we pivoted in a wide turn, the raptidons, with silent, effortless grace, formed into three large V shapes, one formation behind the other.

Rorid eased off close to the fight and let loose a raucous screech. I heard the defiance, the courage, and the confidence in it. No one needed to speak Raptidon to know that Rorid had ordered the attack to begin.

Raptidons dived, then leveled, sailing as smoothly as ships on a breeze. The first V formation led the way, and at the point of that V was Dothram, with Tobble and his raggler.

Woad's embattled men heard and looked up, mouths dropping open in astonishment. Above them more than five hundred raptidons bore down, dark silhouettes appearing out of the morning sun.

I saw the Kazar's archers bend their bows, leaning back to target us, and my heart quickened. They squinted against the nearly horizontal light.

Arrows flew, black darts rising skyward toward the raptidons. Perhaps a hundred arrows in all were launched, but many fell short, and others, slowed by distance, were easy to avoid.

One arrow, however, found its target. It buried itself deep in an aged vulture's wing and he tumbled from the sky, twirling downward. The wobbyk in his talons landed on the upthrusted point of a spear. I couldn't tell what happened to the raggler he must have been carrying.

I gasped at the sickening sight, knowing how much it would discourage the wobbyks.

But I'd forgotten the wobbyk temperament.

It did not discourage them. It enraged them.

As the raptidons moved low over the Dreylander army, wobbyks tossed their ragglers down into the Dreyland shield wall.

I knew that the ragglers were poisonous to most species, but I hadn't understood how their poison worked. As their spikes buried themselves in exposed shoulders and backs, or even on curious upturned faces, I saw why the ragglers were so fearless.

The poison worked swiftly and mercilessly. In just a few seconds, anyone who felt the prick of a raggler spike fell to the ground, writhing and gasping for air.

The Dreylanders were here to burn and kill and destroy. I should have been happy to see them fall. But I couldn't take any pleasure from their suffering.

The raptidons swooped overhead again, and this time they released wobbyks—defiant, fierce wobbyks—just a few feet over the heads of the Dreylanders.

The shield wall, depleted by raggler poisoning, broke and fell back in disarray, into the mass of troops being ripped and scratched and chewed by infuriated wobbyks.

With a great roar, Woad's warriors picked up their shields and advanced in an orderly line, pushing into the broken shield wall, stabbing with spears and swords, hammering with axes and maces.

But the Dreylanders still had greater numbers. And they were well-trained, professional soldiers. They retreated to form a defensive circle around their general.

Worst of all, they had four terramants. Our ragglers would no doubt be useless against them, given the thick carapace covering most of the huge insects' bodies.

Rorid uttered another throaty cry. Rising from the ground, just beyond the village, came a cloud of smaller birds: gulls, ravens, jays, starlings, even little sparrows. They flew fast, tiny wings beating. And to my shock, they went straight for the terramants.

Terramants remind me of massive beetles. Their natural armor shrugs off arrows, spears, and swords. But they have two weak points. One is their underbelly, which is only lightly protected, but nearly impossible to reach.

The other weakness is their eyes—eyes now covered with swarms of small birds, pecking and scratching with fury. One terramant, head bobbing frantically, raced off to the north, as if determined to head home. The other three tried their best to attack. But it's hard to attack an enemy when you're blind.

"It is time," Rorid said. "I will take their general. You will shout a warning if I am attacked from behind. Grip your sword tightly, Byx."

It wasn't a request. It was an order.

We zoomed down out of the sun, Rorid's wings spread wide, the icy wind in my face.

The warriors below must have felt the shadow of the lord of raptidons. They looked up and quailed at the sight. Quailed, but didn't flee.

The Dreylander general was hemmed in on all sides, but his defenders had left a little room so he could see the action over their heads, a circle of space around the large, armored human.

"Now!" Rorid cried, and his talons opened.

I fell, and as I did, I let out a scream that was part fear and part rage.

I landed on wet ground, rolled to soften the impact, and leapt up, muddy, but with my sword drawn. There he was. The general. Twice my height, with a sword longer than my body.

He glared down at me, eyes burning, through a slitted visor. Busy looking at me, he failed to realize that Rorid had flown past, pivoting with acrobatic ease to come at him from behind.

"Kill this . . . this . . . thing!" the general shouted.

Three warriors advanced on me.

Rorid struck. His talons seized the general's helmeted head. I thought he'd pull the helmet off, but I'd underestimated the power of the great raptidon's talons. Rorid squeezed. His huge nails pierced the steel of the helmet, driving deep into the general's head.

"Ahhhhhh!" I cried, and the soldiers advancing on me lost all interest as they spun to attack Rorid.

"Rorid! Behind you!" I shouted.

More Dreylander soldiers rushed to the rescue of their chief. The general's knees buckled. His sword fell from his hand. Out of the corner of my eye, I caught a flash of movement. An archer swiftly nocked his arrow and drew. He wasn't going to miss Rorid, not at this distance.

I didn't think. I acted. I threw my sword.

It wasn't an expert throw. The point didn't bury itself in the archer. But the hilt struck him in the arm and he released his arrow, which flew away harmlessly.

The general fell on his face. Rorid perched on the dead man's head, wings spread for balance.

"Your leader lies dead," Rorid said calmly. "Who wishes to lie beside him?"

27
A Felivet Warrior

Rorid's question was enough to make the advancing soldiers hesitate.

The cry went up on all sides: "*The general is dead!*"

Any fight left in the Dreylanders evaporated. All around me the Kazar's invaders threw down their weapons and raised their hands in surrender.

I stared in stunned disbelief at the carnage. Dead humans. Dead raptidons. Dead wobbyks. Dead ragglers.

Frantically, I searched for Tobble, but I couldn't find him anywhere. A sound rose and grew, the noise of many voices moaning, crying, bellowing in pain or grief. The battlefield had a smell, too, an unforgettable stench composed of blood and fear.

"The day is ours!" Rorid screeched, and from the sky

came an answering cry of fierce exultation from hundreds of raptidons.

He turned his blazing gaze on me. "This is a great triumph for you and your wobbyk compatriots, Ambassador Byx."

"A triumph?" I echoed. "It doesn't feel like a triumph. I was supposed to stop this from happening."

"Did you really think you could stop a war without engaging in war yourself?"

"Khara . . . the Lady of Nedarra seeks peace," I protested.

"All good creatures of any species seek peace, Ambassador." His voice was as gentle as it could be, given the limits of raptidon speech. "And yet war comes. And when it does, there can be only one goal: victory. I suspect the Lady knows this in her heart."

Stepping over bodies and shields, I looked for Tobble, as well as for the felivets I'd seen earlier. Apparently, they'd avoided the fighting, perhaps slipping away during the melee. Interesting, I thought. The valtti Kazar had some felivets, but perhaps they weren't all that interested in dying for him.

A small figure staggered toward me, covered with blood on his face and fur. Tobble!

He was dazed and moving slowly, almost sleepwalking. "Tobble," I cried, "are you hurt?"

"Hurt? No. No, Byx, I'm not hurt."

I'd been through a lot with Tobble. I'd seen his every expression. But the look in his eyes was like nothing I'd ever seen. He didn't seem to be looking at me, but through me.

"The blood . . . ," I said, realizing too late that I was forcing him to explain something he might not want to discuss.

He touched his face, then looked at his fingers, as if mystified. "It's not mine," he said. "It's not mine. I . . . I killed a man, Byx. I could have stopped, you know. He was defeated and I could have stopped. But I didn't, Byx. I didn't stop until he stopped breathing."

Tears spilled from his eyes, cutting channels through the blood. I put my arms around him and held him close. He sobbed and soon my tears joined his.

We'd won.

I wondered if defeat could feel any worse than victory.

Woad's men moved through the dead and wounded, carrying away their injured and ignoring the pitiful pleas of the Kazar's defeated soldiers. Woad had only one doctor in his company, and she was busy cutting off mangled limbs and sewing up great gashes.

The injured Dreylanders cried for water, mostly. Others begged for the mercy of a swift death. Some wept for their mothers.

"Tobble," I said, "we've got to find some waterskins."

Tobble was too confused to argue. I took his paw and

pulled him along with me toward one of Woad's wagons. A big man with just one eye and one arm, a veteran of some ancient battle, stood guard.

"I'm Ambassador Byx," I said to him. "I need waterskins."

"No need." He pointed to a tap in a big barrel. "Just twist it and drink all you like."

"It's not for me," I said. I didn't want to tell him why I needed waterskins. I doubted he would understand.

"For the wounded, then?"

"Yes. Some of the Dreylanders are in need—"

"So you mean the *enemy* wounded?" he interrupted.

"Yes," I answered.

"My name is Gorand," said the guard. He patted his stump with his good hand. "I lost this in battle. I lay in agony forever. You have no idea the thirst of a man who's fought and lost blood."

Gorand paused, lost for a moment in memory. "It was a young warrior who found me still alive. Do you know who he was? The very enemy warrior who'd taken my arm with a well-timed backstroke of his sword. He could easily have finished me off. Instead he gave me water." He shook his head. "I drank it down. No drink since has ever been half as wonderful. When I was done, I asked him why. Why show mercy to a fallen foe?"

"What did he say?" I asked.

"He said the greatest mercy is the one you show to your

enemy. And I've never forgotten. Take all the waterskins you can carry. If anyone challenges you, tell them Gorand sent you."

Tobble and I grabbed three heavy waterskins and made our way across the battlefield. We gave water to the hurt, and to the exhausted, and to those overcome with grief. It was an experience I would never wish on anyone.

I was about to return for more water when I noticed something moving beneath a pile of bodies.

"Come, Tobble," I said. "Help me."

Together, with great effort, we yanked bloodied bodies clear until, at the bottom, we saw a young felivet with a terrible cut down one flank. Her black fur was striped with deep blue, from head to tail.

"Friend felivet, are you thirsty?"

"Friend?" the felivet snarled in what I took to be a female voice. "When have felivets and dogs been friends? Even talking dogs?"

"I'm a dairne, not a dog," I said. "My companion and I are both friends with a felivet named Gambler."

"Gambler is not a felivet name," she muttered. She winced with pain and couldn't stop her pale blue eyes from darting toward the waterskins. But she had the pride of her kind.

"Gambler's what we call him," I said. "But his true name is . . ." I'd only heard it once, and long ago. What *was* Gambler's full name?

Tobble's memory was better than mine. "He told me his true name is Elios Str'ank, Hadrak the Third, Lonko of the Dread Forest."

The felivet blinked. "What did you say?"

"Elios Str'ank, Hadrak the Third, Lonko of the Dread Forest," Tobble repeated. "He said there were more names, but that was plenty to start."

"Your friend is a Lonko of the Dread Forest?" She said it as if I'd announced that natites could fly.

"So he tells us," I said. "And Gambler doesn't lie."

"Although he does tease sometimes," Tobble added, sounding a little more like himself.

"I will have some water, if I may," the felivet said. Tobble sprayed a long stream of water into her rather terrifying mouth. When she was done, she seemed calmer. "I am called Naleese B'del, Lenka of the Urbik River Valley."

Tobble and I introduced ourselves.

"You have been both kind and brave," Naleese said. "But I must ask still more. First, I need a surgeon to sew up this unfortunate wound. Then I would like to be taken to this Lonko of the Dread Forest. I have a message for him, or any felivet in authority."

"Message?"

"Yes. Two messages, in fact. The first was entrusted to me by the Kazar. It urges all felivets in Nedarra to rise up against the Murdano and welcome the rule of the Kazar."

"I don't think Gambler will like that message," I said.

"Nor should he. The Kazar is a monster, a valtti, a traitor to his own people. I was sent with this raid in order to make contact with felivets fool enough to join him. But I carry a very different message, one that does not come from a traitor, but from the oppressed felivets of Dreyland."

"And what is that message?" I asked.

"That," she replied, "will be for the ears of Elios Str'ank, Hadrak the Third, Lonko of the Dread Forest."

28
Gambler's Surprise

Woad's men returned to the mountains, many bandaged, some trying out crude wooden legs. They were able to confiscate all the weapons of the Dreylanders, as well as their horses and provisions. Woad seemed quite pleased.

"You arrived in the very nick of time, Ambassador Byx," he said. "In another ten minutes, we'd have all been dead."

"Thanks should go to Lord Rorid and the wobbyk elders," I said. "Not to mention the ragglers."

"And I do indeed thank them. But it was you who brought raptidon, wobbyk, and raggler together."

I wasn't so sure about that, but it was good to hear. Until Woad went on: "All those dead Dreylanders? You deserve much of the credit, my friend."

He meant it as a compliment, so I nodded and made polite

noises. But my heart dropped like a rock at the thought that he was right.

Rejoining the Army of Peace meant a long ride, and it was neither easy nor pleasant. I'd had to leave poor Havoc back at Bossyp, and my new pony, a little roan lent to me by one of Woad's men, was a grumpy sort, given to sudden bucks and indignant snorts. His name was Taboo, but Tobble nicknamed him "Achoo," because he had a habit of sneezing at odd moments.

Snow fell, then sleet, then more snow. We followed the Telarno River south, so there was always plenty of water, at least. We'd added a large contingent of raptidons, wobbyks, and ragglers, and I knew Khara would be pleased to see the new recruits. But we were a weary, cold, and hungry group, to say the least.

Naleese, the felivet, rode in a wagon for the first two days. On the third, she walked part of the day, and by the time we reached our goal, Naleese was almost back to normal. Still, she never gave any hint of the message she carried for Gambler.

We found the Army of Peace camped at the confluence of the Telarno and its tributary, the River of Reeds, a narrow, slow-moving stream bordered by wetlands and stands of stiff brown cattails.

Sabito spotted us first. "I am told that no less than Lord

Rorid Headcrusher joined you in a terrible fight!" he said, with obvious excitement.

"Yes. In fact, it was Rorid who carried me," I said.

"*Lord* Rorid," Sabito corrected.

"He gave me permission to address him simply as 'Rorid.' You know, among friends there's no need for formality."

Sabito's eyes blazed with envy. "You. You and Rorid Headcrusher, friends. You."

"Tobble and I are very friendly people, Sabito."

He made a sound of disgust. "I can't believe I missed a chance to fly into battle alongside *Lord* Rorid Headcrusher. But once I'd spread the word among our people, the Lady ordered me back here."

"Did Maxyn sail safely?" I asked.

"He did. But whether he arrived at his destination, I cannot say."

"And Renzo?"

"Renzo and Gambler returned with two hundred horses. I am told they even paid for them."

"Shocking."

We were welcomed by one and all, then summoned to Khara's tent. Tobble and I found Renzo and Gambler there, along with General Varis and Bodick the Blue. How good it was to see them all, weary though we were!

Khara gave us each a long hug. She asked how we were. And then she got right down to business. "Tell me everything."

We did. The telling lasted through lunch and into the afternoon. Finally Khara said, "Fine work. But you haven't explained the presence of a felivet in your group."

"She has a message that she'll deliver only to you, Gambler," I said.

His tail whipped the ground. "Me?"

"Yes. We told her your name, and she reacted as if you were someone important."

Gambler licked one of his huge paws. "As if?"

I laughed. "You've always been important to me."

"What name did you give this felivet?"

I had a mouthful of cider, so Tobble answered for me. "Elios Str'ank, Hadrak the Third, Lonko of the Dread Forest. I remembered it!"

"Indeed," Gambler said cautiously. "And her name?"

"Naleese B'del, Lenka of the Urbik River Valley," Tobble recited.

I won't say that Gambler turned pale. Black fur doesn't allow for that. But his eyes went wide and his jaw dropped open, which was at once frightening and funny.

"N-N-Naleese? I mean, the um, the Lenka of the Urbik Valley?"

I stared at Gambler. Tobble stared at Gambler. Tobble and Renzo and I stared at each other. Then we noticed Khara staring at Gambler, so we stared at her. At which point, we all stared back at Gambler.

Was Gambler flustered?

Gambler?

Flustered?

He seemed to expect us to say something. But we were too curious and confused to react. Gambler had actually stuttered. Gambler, the felivet I'd seen, on more than one occasion, charge into near-certain death without seeming even mildly concerned.

"What are you all staring at?" he demanded.

"I think we'd better meet this Naleese," Khara said. She nodded to a soldier, who ran from the tent.

"Well, I have no need to be here," Gambler said, getting up to leave.

Khara shook a finger at him. "I'm afraid I really must insist that you stay."

Gambler's shoulders sagged. His tail dropped to the ground.

Naleese entered behind the soldier who'd retrieved her. Though stitches were visible down her flank, she moved like flowing liquid, a smaller, more lithe version of Gambler.

She dipped her head to Khara. "My Lady Kharassande Donati."

"Welcome, Naleese B'del, Lenka of the Urbik River Valley," Khara said. "Would you like food or drink?"

"No, my lady, I have been very well cared for by your

kind ambassador, Byx of the dairnes."

"I'm glad to hear it. I'm told you have a message. Two, actually."

"I do. The message I was given by the foul valtti who rules Dreyland, along with a message from some of the felivets of Dreyland. The first is a call for all felivets of Nedarra to rise up against the Murdano."

"I see," Khara said. "And the other message?"

Naleese shifted her gaze to include Gambler. "My message is for the ears of the Lonko of the Dread Forest."

Khara nodded. "Gambler, will you hear this message now? Or would you like to withdraw to hear it in private?"

Gambler sighed. "I am happy to share it with you, my lady."

Khara nodded at Naleese.

"I greet you, my long-ago mate," said Naleese, "whom my heart has never forgotten."

Now it was my mouth hanging open. I shot my eyes right. Yes, Tobble was equally shocked. And Renzo. And Khara. And Sabito. And if Havoc had been in the tent, I suspect he'd have been shocked as well.

"I say to you," Naleese continued, "that I treasure our time together on the Isle of Scholars, where we studied philosophy and astronomy." Her voice was low and rough, like a ragged lullaby. "When Tobble of the Bossyp wobbyks spoke your name, I knew I had to speak to you."

Every eye turned on Gambler. "I too . . . treasure . . . our, um, time together."

"I am glad to hear it. It may interest you to know that you have three kits, two female, one male."

"I . . . congratulations?" Gambler managed. He blinked. "That's good. Yes, good. The more young felivets in the world, the better."

"Why, Gambler, you rogue!" said Bodick, slapping her thigh. "You've got yourself some kittens!"

"Kits," Naleese corrected.

"That's what wobbyks call our babies, too," said Tobble. "Also kidlets. And wibbles."

"You didn't know you had children?" Renzo asked, shaking his head.

Naleese answered for Gambler. "It is not the habit of male felivets to involve themselves closely with their offspring."

"Is this your message, then?" Khara asked.

"No, my lady. My message is this. The felivets of Dreyland have been corrupted, manipulated, and used by the valtti who styles himself Kazar. But many good and true felivets resist, and many more would, but for threats the valtti has made against their kits."

Gambler suddenly found his voice. "Does he threaten your . . . our kits?"

"He holds them hostage in his dungeon. My message is

not about that alone, but for all the felivets of Dreyland. All our Lonkos are dead. Only two Lenkas survive, but we are watched constantly. Our people need a leader. Our people need a wise, strong, and good leader. Our people need you, Elios Str'ank, Hadrak the Third, Lonko of the Dread Forest. Will you come to Dreyland? Will you lead us against this valtti usurper?"

"Will I . . . what?"

Khara looked to General Varis, and their eyes met. I could see they were both intrigued by this development.

General Varis said, "What exactly do you propose, Naleese?"

"If the Kazar were dead, or at least out of power, his army would not invade Nedarra. There would be no war."

"The Murdano's navy would still sail," said Bodick.

"We have the word of Queen Pavionne that the natites will stop the Murdano's navy," Renzo said.

Khara held up a hand for silence. We waited while she considered. After a moment, she spoke directly to Gambler.

"Tell me, old friend," she said, "is this a mission you would undertake?"

29
A Farewell

In the evening, we gathered around a fading campfire. It was quite late, and we were all exhausted. But it felt so good to be back together that we couldn't seem to let the night end.

I felt as if I were home, strange as it was to think of an army on the move that way. I was relieved, too, to once again have followed through on Khara's directive. Twice I'd been tasked with diplomacy. And twice I'd accomplished my goal—although not without pain, bloodshed, and tears.

Gambler was stretched out next to me, his belly exposed to the glowing embers.

"I never knew you had children," I said to him. "Kits, I mean."

"Nor did I. As Naleese explained, it is not the custom for males of my kind—for a Lonko—to raise kits—"

"How very convenient," Renzo interrupted.

"But the thought of my progeny in a dungeon..." Gambler shook his head.

"So is Naleese your wife?" Tobble asked.

"We don't form lifelong partnerships," Gambler replied. "That is the way of humans. But she is someone I, well, care for."

"Have you considered that this could be a trap?" Sabito asked from his perch on a tree limb.

"No," I said. "Naleese spoke what she believed to be the truth."

"I have no choice." Gambler sighed. "If it is true that I can raise a force of felivets in Dreyland and stop this monstrous valtti, it is my duty to try. He is a traitor to my kind."

Naleese joined us, almost unnoticed. Like Gambler, she moved silently. She settled near him. Softly he brushed the side of his head against hers. I knew nothing of felivet romance, but it certainly looked to me like a gesture of affection.

"We must go," Gambler said, and Naleese nodded. "But it will be with a heavy heart. I don't know when, or whether, I shall see any of you again."

Tobble pulled the last bite of toasted willowbean from a charred stick. "How will you get across the mountains?"

Gambler laughed. "We are felivets, not wobbyks, Tobble. We will move by night, unseen. We have no need to carry wagons full of supplies. We will hunt as we move." He stretched and stood. "You are ready, Naleese?"

It dawned on me that he meant to leave immediately. "No!" I blurted. "You can't leave tonight."

"Time of is the essence," Gambler said.

"I know, but . . ." I looked at Khara for help, but she just shook her head. "We just got here," I said in a lame voice. "And what about Naleese? She's still recovering."

"I'm fine, Ambassador," she replied. "And we must hurry. Our kits . . ."

"Of course," I said, embarrassed by my selfishness.

Our goodbyes were brief and simple. Felivets distrust sentiment. And we were soldiers of a sort, after all.

Gambler and Naleese moved into the shadows as the rest of us watched.

"Gambler!" I called after him.

He stopped and looked back. His eyes caught the firelight, glowing like tiny yellow moons.

I ran to him. "I've done some foolish things and some wise things, Gambler," I said. "But perhaps the wisest thing I ever did was trust you."

"I might say the same about you," he replied. He gave a little nod. "Be well, my friend."

Within seconds, the two great cats were invisible, as much a part of the velvety evening as the black forest surrounding us.

It was difficult to sleep that night. I heard Tobble shifting in his bedroll and knew that he, too, was awake.

"Do you remember that moment when Gambler turned to face the Knight of the Fire? Alone?" I asked.

"How could I forget?" Tobble sniffled. "And remember all the times he threatened to eat me?"

I laughed. "And yet here you are, safe and sound. His growl was far worse than his bite."

"Sometimes," said Tobble, managing a laugh. "I wonder if I'll ever ride atop a felivet again, Byx."

"I know you will."

"I mean that felivet. *Our* felivet."

"We'll see Gambler again, Tobble. I'm sure of it."

We went on and on, sharing our favorite Gambler stories, as if by talking we could keep him there with us. At last we drifted off, but we weren't asleep for long. It was still dark, though a faint gray light was just rising in the east, when Renzo shook me awake.

"What? Are we under attack?"

"No," Renzo said. "But we have news. The Murdano's navy has left port. It's on its way to the coast of Dreyland."

Tobble and I both sat up, suddenly alert.

"The natites?" I said.

"Yes, the natites will stop them, or at least most of them. Also, Khara's learned that there are gulls in Saguria flying to the Kazar to report on the navy's movement. The Kazar won't know that the ships will never actually reach Dreyland."

"What does that mean for us?" Tobble asked.

Renzo paced, hands clenched behind his back. "The Kazar will only know that the Murdano is attacking. He'll respond by pushing the terramant attack to begin. We have to move, and quickly, to stop them."

I stood. "We leave today?"

"As soon as possible," Renzo answered. "There's very little time. Perhaps too little time."

Within hours, we were off, an entire army moving resolutely toward an uncertain future.

It was not an easy march. I've traveled many difficult paths since being driven from my home. But nothing can compare to the grinding exhaustion of crossing the Perricci Mountains with howling winds and snow up to my chest.

Woad's battered, weary men joined us to act as guides, but they could do nothing for the sickness that came as we climbed higher. It seemed as if our lungs would no longer fill. Each breath was meager. My head hurt constantly. My limbs, often numb, felt as heavy as lead.

Frostbite began to claim victims. Human ears and noses froze. Khara was constantly on the move, first riding, and then walking on snowshoes Woad had provided. She went up and down the beleaguered line of troops, cajoling, reassuring, and inspiring by example. None of the warriors was about to complain or fall out, so long as their young leader could still go on.

It was four days before we crested the ridge. Sabito flew ahead to scout and returned with reassuring news that the terramant outbreak hadn't yet happened. He saw no sign of the Murdano's army.

If the attack by the Kazar's army and the terramants came before the Murdano's troops arrived, we knew we would have to try to stop them ourselves. If the forces of the Murdano and the Kazar ended up confronting each other directly on the Zebaran plains, the Army of Peace could try to get the two sides to negotiate.

Either we would have to fight the Dreylanders alone, or we'd be trapped between two warring armies.

Neither option sounded promising.

We faced three challenges, Khara had told me, what seemed like ages ago. I'd helped with the first two. We had the natites and the wobbyks on our side, not to mention the ragglers and raptidons.

But that was easy. It was diplomacy. Listening. Talking. Persevering.

Would that be enough?

I remembered Khara's words, that night in her tent: "We'll

either stop the war and prevail, or we'll die trying."

If it came to that last challenge—to the fighting—what help could I really be?

I was just a dairne, the runt of my litter.

The one who refused to leap into a silly lake.

I'd been in a few fights since then. Redeemed myself a bit. But in the battle we might well soon face, I'd be useless.

30
Khara's Decision

When we at last reached the highest point in the pass, the sky cleared. The sun caroming off the snow and ice was almost blinding, the air dry but bitter cold. We were boxed in on both sides by steep mountains, and we couldn't yet see our objective, the Zebaran plains, as there were still peaks ahead.

Nonetheless, we found a way to view our goal. Some long-forgotten power had built a tall stone ziggurat in the middle of the pass, a narrow pyramid with a sloping pathway cut into the sides.

Khara invited General Varis, Renzo, Tobble, and me to climb with her. Fortunately, the path was just wide enough to allow our horses to do the hard work of climbing, at least as far as the second platform, a wide space high above the ground.

"What a view!" Tobble exclaimed. "It's like being a rap-tidon!"

"It's amazing," I agreed, as we tied off the horses with feedbags. We rested and refreshed ourselves and added whatever other warm garments we'd not yet donned. At that giddy altitude, even dairne fur was no match for the cutting wind.

From that last platform, perhaps two-thirds of the way up the ziggurat, we proceeded on foot. It wasn't an easy climb for any of us, but Tobble, with his short legs, struggled to keep up.

"Come, friend wobbyk," said General Varis. "Hop aboard my shoulders."

I was struck, not for the first time, by Tobble's ability to charm large, dangerous members of other species. He now counted both a felivet and a fierce human warrior as good friends.

Up we went, dragging ourselves through the unforgiving air, until Khara stopped. With the last of my energy, I plowed on until I was beside her and the others on a small, snow-dusted platform.

Tobble climbed off the general's shoulders and hugged me tightly. "That's a long way down!"

"It is," I said, trying to sound nonchalant, even as I was calculating how long it would take to tumble down the mountain to my inevitable death.

From our perch, we could see a slice of the Zebaran

plains, free of snow. Just beyond lay the mountains where we knew the terramants were tunneling. Soon they would pour out like lava, destroying all in their path.

"Snow comes late to the plains," General Varis told us. "The mountains hold back the weather until later in the year."

Sabito sailed over, landing on a railing. "What have you seen?" Khara asked.

"A force of three dozen soldiers on horses. They wear the livery of the Murdano."

General Varis said a rude word, his eyes blazing. "Cavalry scouts sent out ahead of the main force, no doubt. This isn't good. If they behave the way scouts usually do, then the main force is perhaps a day behind, maybe two at most."

Khara nodded, her face grim. "The Murdano's army has come up from the south through the gap. They must have learned about the planned terramant attack."

"Just as we feared," said Renzo.

"If the terramants break through, there's no power in the world that can stop total war," said General Varis.

"Between the two armies, they'll burn every village, every crop. They'll use the people as thralls." Khara rubbed the back of her neck. "And they'll do worse. I fear for those innocent people. They're like butterflies on an anvil, waiting for a hammer to come down."

"It's a three-day march to the center of the Zebaran plains," General Varis said, his voice oddly subdued.

"By then . . ." Renzo trailed off.

"By then, we'll have failed," Khara said. "Thousands, tens of thousands will die. The land will be drenched in blood."

"Maybe Gambler can turn the tide inside Dreyland," Renzo suggested.

"Maybe," Khara said. "But not in time, not if the terramants break through."

"It seems we have no way to stop them," General Varis said bluntly.

For several minutes, no one spoke, our minds feverish with the horror of what was to come.

General Varis, ever the military man looking to pull off a victory, was the first to offer a suggestion. "The Rebit River runs through the Zebaran plains," he said, pointing. "If by chance the terramants emerged on one side, and the Murdano's army was on the other bank . . ."

"The Rebit's shallow," Khara said. "I've waded there in spots where the water was no higher than my knees. It wouldn't hold back either side."

The general started to respond, but Khara silenced him with a slight gesture. She was deep in thought, her brow creased, eyes straining.

At last she spoke. "General Varis, you said it was a three-day march for our army. How long would it take determined riders on the best horses?"

Tobble and I exchanged a worried look.

General Varis shrugged. "A strong rider bringing spare horses with him might do it in a day."

Khara seemed pleased with his answer. "I seldom give orders, General. In most cases, I'm happy to leave that to you, but this is an order only I can give. I'm going to need two strong horses. They'll carry one human rider." She turned her dark, sorrowful eyes on me. "And provisions for that human and one dairne."

So Khara had a plan. A plan that involved me.

"Byx, you'll ride Taboo," she said.

My heart lurched, but I gave a firm nod. If she wanted me to go, I would, and willingly.

"We call him Achoo," said Tobble, ears quivering. "And you'll need food for one wobbyk as well! If Byx is to be there, then I—"

"Yes, you may go as well, Tobble," Khara interrupted. "As you often surprise us. And I have long since learned that you two are inseparable."

"Who is the human rider?" Renzo asked suspiciously.

"I am," Khara said.

"No, my lady!" General Varis protested. "That would be madness!"

"Well, General," Khara said with a crooked smile, "we're out of sane ideas. Madness is all we have left."

The general pounded the railing with his fist. "You cannot risk yourself!"

"The Army of Peace will follow as quickly as possible, General," said Khara, calmly ignoring his outburst.

Renzo grabbed Khara's arm in a most unsoldierly way. "What can you do by yourself?" he demanded. "It'll be suicide! And accomplish nothing."

"There are children down there, old people, peaceful farmers. I won't abandon them, Renzo," Khara said, as she gently, but firmly, extricated herself from his grip. "It might be possible to negotiate with one side or the other, perhaps both. For that, my truth teller will be necessary."

"But what can you possibly accomplish with just a dairne and a wobbyk?" General Varis's face was ruddy with frustration, or perhaps even anger.

"These two have done very well for us so far," Khara said. She placed one hand on my shoulder, and one on Tobble's. "But I'll have something else as well."

With that, she wrapped the fingers of her right hand, blue with cold, around the hilt of her sword. She pulled out the blade and held it high. It didn't glow—that only happened in moments of battle—but we all understood its breathtaking power.

"I don't know what I can do, General Varis," said Khara. "But I know that I cannot stand idly by. I may be more poacher than lady. And my soldiers may be a young dairne and a little wobbyk." She returned the sword to its humble scabbard. "But remember this, General: I carry the Light of Nedarra."

31
Fear, Your Faithful Friend

We made our way back to the army, and the general instructed his soldiers to set up a campsite in the shadow of a near-vertical stone wall. Khara, Tobble, and I immediately began preparations for our journey. My hands trembled slightly as I packed up, but it wasn't just from the cold. It was anticipation, too. Khara needed my help. And what we were about to do could change the fates of nations.

Worst of all, I was afraid. So afraid. I tried to remember my wise words of advice to Maxyn about overcoming fear. But they were just words. Empty syllables.

This was different. This wasn't just a trip to the natites. Or a speech to the wobbyks.

This time, there was every chance we would never return to our friends.

For her part, Khara seemed perfectly serene. I'd seen this

before with her. Once she made a decision, no matter how difficult, Khara was always at peace.

How did she do it? Wasn't she afraid to die? Afraid, at very least, of the pain that came with death? Why couldn't I find that inner calm? That certainty that my dying would somehow matter?

General Varis, even if he wasn't happy about her choice, appeared to have resigned himself to the inevitable. But Renzo was another story. He galloped off, a scowl on his face, and didn't reappear until it was almost time for us to depart.

Khara, Tobble, and I were in her tent, poring over a map as we discussed last-minute logistics, when Renzo stormed in, breathless and flushed.

"Please," said Khara, "do come in."

"Khara." Renzo's voice was hard. "You can't do this."

I looked at Tobble. "We should, uh . . . go, maybe?"

"Stay," Renzo commanded, with all the authority of General Varis in a particularly foul mood. "Stay and hear this."

"All right then," Tobble murmured, shrinking into a corner.

"Khara." Renzo seemed to realize he was pacing and stopped himself. "This is a suicide mission." He was speaking slowly and carefully. "You will die. Byx and Tobble will die, too. Do you understand what I'm saying to you?"

"I'd say that's pretty clear, yes." Khara wasn't exactly smiling. But she wasn't not smiling, either.

"You understand I have nothing against insane fights or

losing odds." He shrugged. "As a matter of fact, I prefer them. But Khara, that's not what this is."

She crossed her arms over her chest but didn't speak.

"And you know that I love the idiotic risks you're willing to take for a cause you believe in. I love your ridiculous stubbornness. I love . . ." He trailed off.

"I have to do this, Renzo."

He strode over, grabbing Khara by both shoulders. "Then let me go with you. At least let me die by your side."

"Renzo." Khara's voice was so soft I could barely hear it. "No. It's hard enough to know I may be risking the lives of Byx and Tobble. Believe me, if I didn't need Byx, I would never ask her to come. But a dairne could prove vital, and where Byx goes, so goes Tobble, it seems."

"And where you go, so go I."

"No," Khara said simply. "I will not risk your life because you're . . . fond of me."

"Fine, then." Renzo stood motionless, staring into Khara's eyes. "Fine. As you wish, my lady," he said, with sudden formality.

And then, to my surprise—and, I suspect, Khara's—he kissed her. He was gone before she could speak.

Khara looked over at us with a flustered smile. "Don't listen to Renzo," she said, clearing her throat. "There's at least a tiny chance we won't die."

We didn't wait for dawn, instead riding while the moon was high. General Varis gave Khara a chestnut stallion, since her own horse seemed to be favoring its left front leg. I followed on Achoo, with Tobble sitting behind me. We had one spare horse carrying food, water, and oats.

"Your horse's name is Victory," the general told Khara.

"Good name," she said as she tightened the girth on her saddle. "Let's hope it's not ironic."

I'd strapped my shield to my saddle. My sword hung at my side. I was ready.

We were riding to stop a war and almost certainly would not survive. That was the truth I couldn't escape: we were heading to our deaths.

Deaths in a noble cause, but deaths nevertheless.

It was hard not to dwell on the obvious. Everything we'd done, all the risks, all the wild adventures, would, in the end, prove futile. The Murdano's army was advancing into the Zebaran plains. At any moment the terramants would complete their tunnel beneath the mountains and erupt into unprotected Nedarra. The Army of Peace would arrive behind us, too late to help.

It was a recipe for disaster.

Renzo was right, and we all knew it.

Before we left, General Varis consulted with Khara one last time. I tried to listen, but I couldn't concentrate, especially since I could feel Tobble trembling behind me.

"Are you scared, my friend?" I asked.

"Not at all," he said, his voice pinched. "You?"

"Not in the least," I said. I twisted to look at him, and we both began to laugh. It was nervous laughter, certainly. Very nervous. But laughter nonetheless.

As we headed off, General Varis, Bodick the Blue, and Renzo stood together, faces grave, watching us begin our descent. All three saluted.

The farther we went, the less brutally cold was the air. The wind died out, so the clouds of steam coming off the horses formed delicate pockets of mist. We rode through them the way Rorid had cut through the clouds.

"Huh," I said. It was the first word any of us had uttered in perhaps two hours.

"Huh? What 'huh'?" Tobble demanded. He was grumpy because I'd awakened him.

"There are four elements that make up all we know, right?"

"You woke me for this? I was having the most delicious dream about blue beetle soup."

I ignored Tobble. "They are, of course, fire, soil, water, and wind. So here's what I've been thinking. We fought the Knight of the Fire. We fell into the terramant tunnel in the soil. The voyage to meet Queen Pavionne was our passage through water. And flying with Rorid, we learned the nature of the air."

"Let's hope we don't ride into more fire," Tobble muttered.

Khara turned in her saddle. "I was taught that there's a fifth element."

"A fifth?" I frowned.

"Spirit. We get warmth and light from fire. We get grain and fruit from the soil. From water comes all life, because without water, what can grow? The air gives us breath and lets us see the world. But it's spirit that unites them all. Fire, soil, water, and wind have no meaning if we don't understand them. It's spirit that gives us understanding, and curiosity, and courage."

"So we're taking this deadly trip to learn about spirit?" I asked.

Khara laughed. "Perhaps so, Byx. We'll certainly need courage."

"I'll leave the courage to you, my lady," Tobble said, still sounding grumbly. He'd had nothing to eat in many hours, and wobbyks do love their meals. "I'll be the spirit of cowardice and fear."

"Are you afraid, Tobble?" Khara's voice was gentle, not reproachful.

"If Byx weren't here, I'd tell you I'm not afraid," Tobble said. "But here she is, and so my lady, yes, I'm very afraid."

"Me too," said Khara. "It's good to be afraid when you're riding into danger. Fear keeps you sharp. It helps you stay alive."

"But you ignore your fear," I protested.

"Never. Fear's the little fairy sitting on your shoulder whispering 'take care' into your ear. Courage isn't fearless-ness. Fear's your faithful friend, Byx, so long as you don't make one great mistake."

"Mistake?"

Khara reined Victory in just a little. The path was wider and we were able to ride side by side. "Never let yourself be afraid of being afraid."

Tobble and I considered Khara's words as we trotted between sparse trees.

"I don't recall," Tobble finally said, "our friend Khara being quite so wise before she became a great lady."

Khara gave a rueful laugh. "It's true I'm no more wise, Tobble," she admitted. "But when people call you 'the Lady,' they tend to forget that fact."

"Wobbyks have a saying," Tobble said. "'Grow tall as a sapling, not tall as a weed. One is watered, the other cut down.' It means—"

"It means," Khara interrupted, "that you can set yourself up as greater than others, but only if you're a tree that gives shade. Not if you're a useless plant that must be cut down."

"Why . . . that's right," Tobble said.

"You see?" I said. "She really has become wise."

Wise, yes, I thought. And courageous enough for all of us put together.

And yet, for all her wisdom, Khara didn't have a dairne's nose. She hadn't yet discovered what I already knew.

We were being followed by a human on horseback.

32
Ambush

The sun rose and we found ourselves crossing rolling foot-hills, able at last to press forward at speed. Forests grew to our east and west, but we followed a path that led through lands cleared for farming, stubbled fields of harvested wheat and rye.

We stopped briefly to water the horses and quickly eat a bite ourselves. It was too early for even farmers to be up, or so we thought, until we heard the lowing of cows anxious to be milked.

"Let's ride on, hopefully unnoticed," Khara advised. "We can't stop to chat with every passing villager." But as we left the road to circle past a small village, Tobble spotted smoke coming from a stone tower. It was quite a considerable fire, a whole bale of hay aflame.

"They're warning other villages," Khara said.

"Warning them of what?" I asked.

"Us. These are people who know little of the world beyond their own village. They've got no reason to trust strangers, certainly not strangers with swords."

I thought nothing more of it until we'd moved on and noticed another signal fire near the next village. As we approached, we saw a thin line of a dozen men and women standing across the path. Most carried staves and pitchforks. One old man had a sword. A middle-aged woman held a long pike.

Khara reined in. "Good morning."

The man with the sword stepped forward. "Who are you that bids us good morning?"

I spoke up. "This is the Lady of Nedarra. She leads the Army of Peace."

"Haven't heard of it," he said. "But we've yet to see an army that didn't take our crops and burn our village."

"You're wise to be cautious," Khara said. "The danger is real, though it doesn't come from us. The army of the Murdano has entered the Zebaran plains. And an army of terramants and soldiers that serves the Kazar of Dreyland may come as well. War is almost upon us. You'd be smart to hide your harvest in deep places in the forest. Your people, too."

By late morning we were on the plains at last, foothills and mountains finally behind us. We were exhausted, but as we followed the river, we felt cheered by the musical noise of water tumbling over rocks—and relieved that our waterskins could be refilled.

We paused to let the horses drink from the river and munch some green shoots still poking through the mud.

Khara seemed in good spirits, in spite of the tension in the air. "We've done well to get this far so quickly," she said, stroking Victory's mane, "but—"

An odd whirring sound cut through the air. Tobble and I had been checking Havoc's shoes for stones, and it took me a second to turn and see why Khara had stopped talking.

Her eyes were wide and startled.

An arrow had planted itself in Khara's chest.

She raised a hand to touch the shaft of the arrow, as if to confirm it was real, and then she cried, "Take cover!"

The words were barely out of her mouth before more arrows flew. One hit Achoo in the haunch. Another struck Tobble's waterskin.

Khara dropped to her knees. I leapt for her and seized her belt, pulling her after me, although there was nowhere to hide.

My shield, still strapped to Achoo, took a hit from yet another arrow. The shaft quivered, but the arrowhead did not seem to reach his hide.

It was all happening so fast. I tried to locate the source of the attack but couldn't place it. I assumed the enemy was in a little patch of trees nearby. But then I caught the flash of more arrows and realized we were under attack from the river.

A skiff powered by two oarsmen was mid-river, coming downstream. Two others, a man and a woman, rode with them. Not soldiers, I didn't think. Bandits.

I had an instinct that they weren't just planning to commit murder and steal our horses but might have spotted something even more valuable: a dairne.

If so, they'd try not to mar my fur with a great bloody hole.

I dropped to the ground, shielding Khara as best I could. The boat nosed into the bank and the man leapt out first, drawing a sword. The woman, carrying a large bow and quiver of arrows, followed.

"Careful of the pelt!" the man warned, confirming my theory.

They'd be on us in ten seconds. I brandished my small sword, and I knew Tobble would launch a crazed attack when they were close enough, but they weren't fools. They spotted Tobble and must have been familiar with the danger posed by an enraged wobbyk.

"Kill the wobbyk," the swordsman ordered. The woman nocked an arrow.

Behind me, I heard the thunder of hooves. More bandits, I assumed in despair.

But I could see that neither of our attackers assumed any such thing, as they moved to face a new threat.

A huge bay horse charged at full gallop. "Khara!" Renzo cried.

He spurred his horse right over the swordsman, knocking him into the mud. The man clambered up and stood his ground, weapon at the ready. Renzo favored his right hand, and the swordsman shifted to stay on Renzo's left, hoping to cut a thigh or perhaps stab upward into Renzo's side.

But Renzo shifted his weight as well. Tossing his sword sideways, he caught it in his left hand and plunged his blade into the man's chest.

Renzo reined in, shaking his bloody sword at the woman and her two oarsmen. "Come on, cowards! Come and test me!"

They chose not to.

The woman dashed back to the boat, and, working their oars feverishly, the bandits returned to the current.

Without a pause, Renzo leapt from his horse and fell to his knees beside Khara.

33
All We Knew to Do

Tobble and I could only watch as Renzo worked with practiced speed. He drew his knife and cut Khara's leather jerkin away from the arrow shaft.

"Water. Clean cloth. Then start a fire. Tobble, do you recognize sorcerer's ear?"

"I do!" Tobble cried, and ran toward the riverbank.

With fumbling fingers I handed Renzo a waterskin, then pulled my blanket from my saddlebag. I ripped a section with my teeth, trying to hold back the tears and keep despair from overwhelming me.

My friend, Khara!

Our only hope for peace in this sorry world.

The blood pumped from the hole in her chest. Her

teeth chattered as Renzo packed the strip of blanket around the wound.

"I ordered you to stay behind," Khara murmured.

Renzo forced a smile. "Did you?"

He spilled water around her wound to see it more clearly, but the blood returned instantly. "Bring me an arrow!" he snapped.

I raced to pull one from the dead archer's quiver. "Here."

Renzo used his stretched fingers to measure the length of the arrow's shaft. Then he examined the arrowhead.

"It's barbed," he said. "And at least three inches have penetrated."

Khara's eyes fluttered, and for a moment I thought she would lose consciousness.

"Hey!" Renzo yelled. "Stay awake!"

"I . . . try . . . ," Khara whispered, her voice slurred.

Tobble came running back, wheezing. He was trailing a green vine. "Here you go."

Renzo stripped the leaves until he had a half dozen. He rubbed them between his palms until they'd turned to a fibrous green paste.

"All right," said Renzo. "Quiet, everyone. I have theurgy to perform."

With his hands enclosing the wound, Renzo shut his eyes and began to rock slowly back and forth. He spoke words I didn't know, in a language I'd never heard.

Eskimin raz dur
Eskamin fell yar
Durin elias
Elias lofel.

He repeated the chant three times, as a strange look of peace transformed Khara's face.

Renzo opened his eyes and looked over at us. "She'll be out for a while. That way, she won't feel what's next."

Tobble gulped. "What's next?"

"Get me a flat stone that will fit in my hand," Renzo said, by way of answer.

I knew what was coming. Khara had saved my life after I'd been hit by a poacher's arrow.

I found a flat stone and hurried back with it.

"Help me prop her up," Renzo said. Tobble and I heaved Khara into a seated position, and Renzo used her knife to cut off part of the shaft, leaving six inches protruding.

"Listen to me, you two." We were listening. "Tobble, here, take some of the sorcerer's ear. Byx, when the arrowhead moves, you grab it carefully and pull it through."

With that, Renzo took the flat stone and hammered it into the shortened end of the shaft. It took a second blow before the arrowhead cut through Khara's back and emerged below her shoulder blade. Blood spilled and my hand was slippery, but I pinched the arrowhead with my fingers and drew it out enough to let me grab the shaft itself.

I had to pull hard to get it through. When it came free, I stumbled back. Tobble moved nimbly to stuff the bleeding hole with the green herb.

"Get the blanket under her," Renzo snapped. "And get a fire going. Now!"

I've never struck a flint with more concentration. Thankfully, there was no breeze and my small store of kindling caught flame quickly. Tobble was already dragging fallen branches back. Before long we had a decent fire blazing.

Renzo laid Khara's knife into the flames. I shuddered. I knew what he was planning.

"She'll wake from the spell soon," he said. "I'd rather do this before she does. It'll be painful."

Khara shifted. She was already shaking off the dulling effects of the spell. It took several more minutes before the blade was hot enough for Renzo's purposes.

"Hold her down, you two," he instructed. "Then, when I say to, heft her up again."

Tobble and I nodded.

"Almost done," Renzo said to Khara. He pressed the red-hot blade flat against the entry wound. The sound of burning skin was like bacon in a pan.

Khara jerked rigid and screamed through gritted teeth.

"Lift her!"

We did, and he placed the other side of the knife against

the wound in her back. This time Khara's cry was muffled, her face buried in Renzo's shoulder.

When he released her, she'd lost consciousness.

Renzo sat back, looking haggard and exhausted. The three of us were covered in Khara's blood.

"Listen, Byx and Tobble," said Renzo. "You've done well. Now I need you to keep watch so that we're not surprised. Keep the fire fed. And hobble the horses, we'll need them. I know I'm asking a lot, but I won't be able to help."

I wanted to ask why, but he'd already begun to rock back and forth, whispering his strange incantations.

For six hours, Tobble and I kept our senses sharp. We hauled wood, fed the tired horses, and waited in anxious silence as Renzo chanted without stop.

The sun was falling when Renzo at last collapsed onto his back. I ran to him. "Are you all right?"

"Just exhausted. I've given all I have. I just don't know if it's enough, Byx."

His lids dropped and he fell instantly into a deep sleep beside Khara. We covered them both with what blankets we had.

It was all we knew to do.

34
War Approaches

Tobble and I took turns keeping watch all night. We'd seen nothing of concern—no villagers, no bandits, no scouts—but every sound set us on edge.

Renzo woke at dawn. Khara had barely moved. "How do you think she's doing?" I asked as he felt her forehead for fever.

He took a moment to consider, rubbing his jaw. When he answered, he kept his voice low so that only Tobble and I could hear. "I have the theurgy I picked up as a thief, but healing's not my specialty. If the wound doesn't fester, she'll probably survive. But it will be a while before her sword arm is useful. She may never regain its full strength."

Tobble passed Renzo a mug of tea. "Is there any chance," he began, "I mean, with just the four of us, and with Khara wounded . . . is there any chance we could, um, prevail?"

Renzo gave a humorless laugh. "There was never more than the slimmest of chances. And now there's still less." He looked over at me. "I can't lie to a dairne."

Khara awoke, moaning with pain, a few minutes later. She drank a small amount of water and then, her voice a mere whisper, said, "We must ride."

"Already you're giving orders?" Renzo said, but he was clearly overjoyed to hear her voice.

"We've no time to lose," said Khara. Her face was drawn, her clothing stained with her own blood, but her determined gaze told us not to argue. In any case, we knew she was right.

We packed up silently. The night before, Tobble and I had managed to remove the arrow from Achoo's haunch and sew up the wound. But my poor pony was limping a little, and I switched to one of the packhorses in order to leave Achoo unburdened.

For her part, Khara insisted on riding solo. After some argument, Renzo relented and lifted Khara onto Victory. To our amazement, she managed to stay upright, but just barely. Renzo took the lead, with Khara just behind. Now and then, she drifted off to sleep, so Tobble and I rode alongside Victory to keep an eye on her. We rode hard, even when Khara uttered cries of pain. She hadn't given up, it seemed, but Renzo's expression was grim.

The countryside was eerily calm. Humans had long lived in this part of the world, and they'd taken great care of their land. The fields were plowed into perfectly straight lines, surrounded by ditches to carry away heavy rains. I saw well-tended wooden fences, low barns, and paddocks. The villages had no walls. No armed men. This was a land that had been at peace for many years.

Now, war was coming and we were its harbingers. I felt dirty somehow, bringing my sword and shield to this tranquil place.

We rode north, toward the area where we expected the terramant attack to unfold. When we reached the top of one of the infrequent hills, we noticed a dark smudge on the horizon behind us. Renzo, more experienced in such things, frowned.

"That would be the Murdano's army."

Khara merely nodded in agreement.

It took all day to reach our goal. "By morning the army will catch up to us, if not sooner," Renzo said. "We'll need to lie low. There'll be no fire tonight."

We found a knot of thorny bushes beside the river and decided to camp there. As darkness descended, the campfires of the Murdano's army flickered like fireflies—hundreds of them, maybe more, perhaps a half league distant. Their soldiers would be cooking stew and brewing tea, sleeping in tents after warming themselves by their fires.

We still had plenty of provisions, so we ate well enough, but we spent a damp, cold night with the three of us huddling around Khara to give her what warmth we could.

In the morning I woke to the prodding of a toe in my back.

"Huh?" I said. "What?"

I glanced up to see Khara. She looked ghastly. Her face was drained of color. Her cheeks were sunken. Her hair was matted. But she was standing on her own, hands on hips.

We drank water from the river and ate a quick, cold breakfast of parched oats. As we readied to leave, a raptidon floated high overhead. I nudged Renzo and we watched for a moment, afraid the hawk might be a spy for the Murdano. But as he circled lower, Tobble cried, "It's Sabito!"

Sabito landed on a bush. He took one look at us and demanded, "What has happened?"

"The Lady was attacked by bandits," I explained. "She was wounded."

We gave a brief account. We were in a hurry, and so was he. "Even with your inadequate eyes," said Sabito, "you have seen the Murdano's army, no doubt?"

"Yes." Renzo nodded. "We know."

Sabito cocked his head. "But you continue?"

"We follow the Lady's orders," Renzo replied.

"When it suits you," Khara said, managing the ghost of a smile.

"My lady, forgive me, but this is lunacy," Sabito exclaimed. "We must get you to a safe village and let you heal."

"No village is safe now," Khara said. "If the Murdano's deprived of battle, he'll let his men loose to pillage. Yes, even his own people."

Sabito didn't argue. "General Varis has driven the Army of Peace hard, without letup, but they are still a day's travel away."

"The Murdano hasn't spotted them yet?" Khara asked.

"No, my lady. The Murdano sent a flock of razorgulls to spy out the countryside but, well, some friends of mine and I took care of those flying rats."

"Good," Khara said. Her voice was a hoarse shadow of itself. "That was well done, Sabito. And now I have to ask more from you."

"What service can I render, my lady?"

"Can you fly on ahead and come straight back at the first sight of terramants emerging?"

"Of course," Sabito replied. "And happily."

"Then fly, my friend. Time is short. And hope dwindles."

Sabito took wing immediately. "Saddle up," Khara commanded.

"Khara—" Renzo started to argue.

Khara held up a hand. "Don't make me use what little strength I have left to debate you, Renzo."

We returned to our mounts and moved on. It was nearing noon when a speck appeared in the sky: Sabito, flying with all his speed. He didn't even bother to alight, simply screeching over our heads, "The terramants! They've broken through! The Kazar's army is right behind them, cavalry and foot! They're moving fast."

We rode at full speed. Behind us, we could clearly see the Murdano's army. The terramant breakout grew clearer, too, a widening hole in the low slope of the mountain. Dark shapes, like mere ants from this distance, rushed out onto the plains.

The Kazar's forces and those of the Murdano raced to cover the miles that separated them, two great armies intent on slaughter. The war between Dreyland and Nedarra was about to begin.

35
On the Brink

Sabito continued to take stock of the gloomy situation, hovering alongside Khara to report on everything he found. Behind us, he said, came twenty thousand of the Murdano's men on foot, along with another three thousand mounted cavalry, platoons of archers, and powerful beasts pulling siege towers, trebuchets, and war wagons.

Rushing toward us from the north were thousands of terramants, an insect swarm devouring crops and farmers alike, destroying all they came near, and behind them, far closer than we had expected, came the mass of the Dreyland forces.

Fleeing refugees began to reach us, many injured and all terrified, carrying what few possessions they'd managed to gather. They drove their animals and bundled their children onto carts, moving as fast as they could. They couldn't know that they were rushing toward a Nedarran army that might treat them no more gently than the Dreylanders.

This peaceful, bucolic place was about to become a land of horrors.

"Sabito!" Khara called. When he swooped near, she asked, "Do you see the Murdano himself with his army?"

"Judging by the great platform being carried on the backs of a hundred thralls, I'd say yes."

"Now, Sabito." Khara winced as she shifted position on Victory. "Go see whether the Kazar is present with his troops."

Sabito flew off and Renzo asked, "What are you looking for?"

Khara shook her head. "Just curious."

I heard the lie. But I said nothing.

Sabito soon returned to report that the Kazar was with his army. "Unless," he added, "there is some other huge gray felivet surrounded by terrified thralls."

"Can you estimate where the armies will meet?" Renzo asked.

"There is a small village ahead, perhaps a quarter league. I do not know its name, but a blue jay I encountered says the surrounding area is called Soraskivelt. It is an ancient tongue. The name means 'Field of Slaughter.'"

"So glad I asked," Renzo muttered.

"Long centuries ago, a great battle was fought there," Sabito explained, staying perfectly level with us as we galloped.

"There are burial mounds to the west, and stone altars closer to the village."

"Then I know what I must do," said Khara. She shaded her eyes and peered into the distance. "Let's hope that by day's end, this field will have earned a happier name."

None of us believed that would happen. But we kept going, pushing our poor horses for all the speed they could manage. We were soon met with great burial mounds on our left, some as high as ten humans.

"What an odd way to honor the dead," Tobble remarked.

"Oh? And how do wobbyks do it?" I asked.

"Why, the sensible way, of course. When we die, we're dropped into a tar pit."

In no way did that sound superior to a burial mound, but I kept my mouth shut.

"Look!" Renzo cried, pointing.

The terramant front crested a low hill in the distance, surging like an incoming wave. It wasn't a line, exactly. More like a disorderly cavalry charge of gigantic insects, all of them many times my size.

The Murdano's army had spotted them, too. They rushed to form ordered infantry squares, creating a kind of massive, moving chessboard. The squares were perhaps ten warriors on each side, with more on the interior and three officers on horses at the center. Most of the fighters were armed with huge silver spears. A triple line of archers ran behind the first row of squares.

"What are they doing?" Renzo asked, jerking his chin at a group of thralls pounding big wooden stakes into the ground.

"They'll fire barbed crossbow bolts at the terramants," said Khara, "with ropes connected to the stakes, hoping to tie the terramants down."

"Will it work?" I wondered aloud.

Khara gave no answer, instead shifting her gaze to the Dreylander forces. The fighters were forming a line of their own, six or seven terramants deep. Behind this terrifying assault force stood large ranks of spearmen. And behind them was a gaudy, wheeled palanquin drawn by thralls in rough hemp harnesses, on which a huge felivet paced back and forth.

The Kazar. The valtti traitor to his people.

At the far ends of the Nedarran line, I could just make out some Knights of the Fire. I counted only six, but as we all knew from personal experience, these knights were more dangerous than any mortal man. Living fire, sentient and lethal, dripped from their lowered lance points. No doubt it would be used against the terramants, who were difficult to kill with blades but had no defense against fire.

The Nedarran forces began to chant: *Murdano! Murdano!*

On the other side, an answering howl rose, human voices

combined with the bizarre clicking sounds made by the terramants.

Khara drew a deep breath. "Are you ready, boy?" she whispered to Victory, who nickered his response.

To her left was the Dreylander's line. To her right was the army of the Murdano. The path ahead was clear. And hopeless.

The air seemed to tremble with anticipation and dread. Khara turned Victory away from the battle to face us.

"My friends, this isn't the final act I'd hoped for. I wanted a chance to speak to the Murdano and the Kazar. With one hand, I meant to threaten them with the Army of Peace, and with the other hand, to offer them a brighter future. But our army is still too far away, so I must take a different path."

"Khara...," Renzo said. But he had no argument to make, beyond saying her name.

"Whatever happens, you must look to your own safety. That's my order to you, and you *will* obey me." She put some steel into that command. "You are each very dear to me. I'll gain courage from believing that you're ... alive."

"Khara," Renzo said again, pleading. "Your right arm, your sword arm, is too weak."

"He's right," I said.

"No arm is weak," said Khara, "that wields the Light of Nedarra."

Renzo closed his eyes. Tobble wiped away a tear.

"My fate is mine alone," Khara said. "Know that I love each of you." She added a look that was just for Renzo. "Though in different ways."

With that, Khara turned her horse to face the coming battle. "Well then, Victory. Let's see if you live up to your name."

Victory leapt forward, as the Lady of Nedarra rode alone toward the killing ground.

Or at least she would have been alone, if my packhorse, Doona, hadn't mistaken the dead branch near his right hoof for a snake. He whinnied in terror and did what any frightened horse would do under the circumstances: he followed the mighty steed galloping away.

Khara rode on. And Tobble and I rode just behind her.

36
Khara's Challenge

As the two armies neared each other, they slowed, organizing for battle, the opposing generals moving units like toys.

On our right sat the bristling porcupine of Nedarran squares. On our left, the endlessly restive terramants, grinding their enormous jaws. The space between the armies, a muddy patch of land with graying grass, had tightened. A length of perhaps fifty horses separated them.

Khara rode to the very center and brought Victory to a halt. She heard Doona's hoofbeats and turned, realizing for the first time that Tobble and I were with her.

I was afraid she might be furious, but she simply nodded at us, as if we'd agreed on some secret pact. I supposed she'd finally accepted that fate would be including a useless dairne and wobbyk in her grand, suicidal gesture.

Khara's cheeks were hollow, her eyes glazed with pain.

She held her right arm close. I saw a bright red spot on her jerkin, where blood from her wound had escaped its bandage. Still, she rose in her stirrups and found a voice I had never heard from her before. In the puzzled silence that greeted her arrival, the sound carried far.

"Hear me, armies of Nedarra and Dreyland. I am Kharassande Donati, the Lady of Nedarra, leader of the Army of Peace, which approaches with eager warriors and fresh horses."

Heads turned, checking to see if this third army was already in view.

"I come with an offer of peace," Khara said. "None of you wish to die, but die you will, if the decision is left to your corrupt and foolish leaders. You will die for them! For a mad, renegade felivet. Or for a weak and greedy tyrant who's made himself the enemy of all living things."

The armies were listening. The humans, at any rate. I couldn't read the terramants.

"I know that you terramants serve the Kazar," Khara continued, "only because he has seized control of your food supplies and threatened you with starvation."

Now I was certain the terramants were listening. It must have worried the Kazar, for I saw a horseman racing from his palanquin to the front line. From gestures alone, it was clear that the horseman was delivering a taste of the Kazar's anger and threats.

But the Murdano wasn't happy, either, at the prospect of losing his chance at a war. Suddenly, from the Nedarran ranks, an arrow flew.

"Look out!" Tobble screamed, and my heart lurched.

Khara kneed Victory, who turned instantly. Grimacing, she drew her sword and batted the arrow away.

"Do not obey these evil leaders!" Khara said. But I could see, as she no doubt could, that the officers were beginning to regain control of their fighters. At any moment, a trumpet could sound, signaling a charge.

"I invoke the ancient rituals of combat!" Khara said. "In times of old, when two armies met, the leaders of each side could avoid slaughter by agreeing to a fight between champions, a single warrior from each side. I challenge the Murdano and the Kazar! I challenge them to single combat. And if they are not cowards—I say again, *if* they are not cowards—then let them come forth and fight me! Surely these two great leaders cannot be afraid of a mere girl."

Hearing her words, I felt a mixture of pride and terror. She was so brave, our Khara. And so foolish.

The first response came in a felivet roar so loud that the ground seemed to shudder. The front rank of terramants opened and there, not more than three felivet leaps away, was the Kazar.

He was the gray of rain clouds, with black stripes on his face. And he was huge, half again as big as Gambler. When he whipped his long tail, I saw that it ended in a silver blade almost the length of, well, me. And when he extended his claws, they, too, glistened silver, adding metal to the terror of felivet claws.

"Do you challenge me, girl?" the Kazar roared. "I will eat you while you still live! And when I'm done with you, I'll do the same to this so-called Murdano!"

The attention of all shifted toward the Nedarran side. I half expected to see the Murdano come swaggering into view. But he had the choice of whether to accept combat himself or name a champion. Coward that he was, he chose the latter.

A hideous creature strode toward us past the Nedarran squares, as archers stepped aside to allow him passage. He was huge, no less than seven feet tall, and though he walked on two legs like a man, he wasn't human, or at least not entirely so.

His arms were so long that his fingers, each ending in a curved claw, dragged on the ground. His legs were short but powerful, like tree trunks. He wore shining silver armor that failed to conceal the oddly misshapen form beneath, too long in the body, too short in the legs.

But it was something else that sent a shock of fear through all who saw it. Fangs protruded from beneath his lipless muzzle. He had the head, unmistakably, of a cobra.

The sight was so horrifying that at first I didn't notice,

just a few steps behind the creature, the Murdano himself. He looked as I remembered him, young, with ebony hair and a trim beard. He wore a quilted doublet covered by gleaming, golden chain mail.

"Gaze upon my champion!" the Murdano cried. "I present Chimera!"

37

A Mad Kitten and a Cowardly Man

I shot a look at Khara, expecting to see the cold fear I was feeling. Instead her expression was one of pure contempt.

"I call you coward!" Khara yelled. Her voice was weakening, but it was still resolute. "You and your wizards have created this abomination, even as you plot the destruction of every species that refuses to bow to you."

The Murdano wasn't impressed. "I showed you mercy once, girl, but there'll be none today. Chimera will destroy you, and then do the same for the mad kitten over there who calls himself Kazar."

I looked to the Kazar to see how he'd react to this taunt, but he was distracted by a felivet who seemed to be whispering in his ear.

I could barely control my shock.

I knew the felivet whispering so confidentially to the Kazar.

Gambler? Had Gambler betrayed us?

Naleese was there, too. Around their necks, both wore gold chains, featuring filigree badges with the letter *K*.

K for Kazar. The same insignia his personal armed guards wore on their uniforms.

"Byx," Tobble whispered.

"I see."

"He wouldn't," Tobble murmured. "He couldn't."

I refused to believe it was possible.

Khara raised her voice again. "Warriors of Dreyland, will you die for a leader who's an outcast among his own people, a despised valtti? A felivet gone mad? A felivet who wouldn't hesitate to make a meal out of any of you?

"And you, warriors of Nedarra. What has this cowardly man, this Murdano, ever done for you, for your families, for your villages? He takes your wealth to fight his wars and lays waste to the land, killing all who will not accept servitude. He's an enemy to every nonhuman species, and an enemy to humans as well."

"She's right, Nedarrans," roared the Kazar. "You see my army! Will you be food for my terramants?"

"You fool," the Murdano replied. "You don't realize that as we speak my navy approaches your shores. I will burn your palaces and slaughter your people!"

"Actually . . ."

The word was out of my mouth before I could stop it. I

cast a mortified look at Khara, but she nodded very slightly, urging me to continue.

"Actually," I repeated, loudly this time, "the natite queen Pavionne has promised that no Nedarran navy will reach Dreyland."

"You lie!" the Murdano screamed.

"I was taken by underwater craft to speak with Queen Pavionne on behalf of my lady. The queen won't tolerate the slow rain of drowned bodies falling on her city."

The Murdano swallowed hard and glanced at Chimera for reassurance. Chimera's forked tongue flicked out and back, out and back.

"Then victory is assured!" the Kazar exulted. "I must thank you, girl, and your talking dog as well. Without his navy, this pitiful creature, this weak and cowardly Murdano, will soon be chained to my castle walls, dying a very slow, very painful death."

Behind the Kazar, I noticed that Gambler and Naleese had been joined by a younger male felivet with spotted fur.

"Before you two begin your war," said Khara, "you will first have to go through me."

"You?" the Kazar demanded. "I'll eat you as a midmorning snack. What are you, fool of a human girl, that you would challenge me?"

"I rule this land. It's me she challenges," the Murdano shouted furiously. "But I ask the same question. Who are you,

you nobody, you nothing, you ridiculous child who threatens me with an imaginary army?"

Both armies howled, taunting Khara. She sat silent, head bowed, until they'd had their fun. Then she nodded, as if in agreement.

"Who am I? I am Kharassande of the House Donati. And one thing more. I am she who wields"—she paused, drew her sword, and held it high in the air—"the Light of Nedarra!"

At that, the blade revealed itself. It blazed with light so dazzling that many turned their eyes away.

"And it's with this sword, and in the name of the free people of all species and all lands, that I will fight you, valtti, and the coward's abomination too, and bring an end to your war and to your reigns!"

That was enough for the Kazar. He coiled his muscles and leapt.

He didn't just leap. He flew.

It wasn't a felivet leap, amazing as those are. It was more than muscle and grace: it was theurgy. The force that holds all things to the earth simply seemed to stop working, as the Kazar flew thirty feet and came arcing down toward Khara.

He was as big as Victory. I saw his underbelly soar above me. I saw his claws extended, and his raging yellow eyes.

How could Khara sit astride her horse so calmly?

How could Victory resist rearing and running away?

The Lady of Nedarra watched the great cat, calculating

the right instant to urge Victory forward. It was just a few feet, but enough that the Kazar flew harmlessly overhead. He landed with the smooth ease of his species and spun around.

His back was to Chimera, and the reptilian creature saw his chance. He bounded forward, raising a short spear high overhead, aiming to plant it in the Kazar's back.

"Dieeeee!" Chimera hissed.

The Kazar, caught off balance, twisted aside, but not far enough. Chimera's sharp blade sliced a red line down the Kazar's flank.

The felivet valtti forgot all about Khara. Good, I thought, let the two murderers kill each other. But that wasn't Khara's plan. She urged Victory forward into the space between Chimera and the cat.

"Hold!" she cried.

Chimera and the Kazar were both so startled that they obeyed. They weren't alone in their surprise. A ripple of astonishment rolled through both armies.

"Before you fight each other," Khara said, "fight me."

"No, Khara," I whispered. "No."

The murmur of astonishment became one of pity. I heard variations on the phrase "she's gone mad," whispered on both sides.

"And to give you some chance, however small," Khara added, "I'll take you both on at once."

38
A Small Girl on a Big Horse

The crowd fell silent.

A small girl on a big horse, accompanied by only her "dog" and a wobbyk, had just insulted two of the most dangerous creatures ever to walk this world.

"Fight me first. Let's see which of you two great beasts has the courage and skill to take me on," Khara said. "Then, if either of you survives . . ." She shrugged, and both armies laughed nervously. "Do you accept my challenge? Remember that my dairne companion will know if you lie."

"I will happily kill you first," the Kazar said, with exaggerated courtesy.

"Not if I do it!" Chimera shouted, lunging at Khara. He'd almost certainly have thrust his spear into her heart, if the Kazar hadn't extended a lightning-quick paw to trip the monster.

Chimera fell facedown in the mud.

The Kazar rushed at Khara. I gasped.

Khara spoke a word to Victory, who dropped his head to the ground. She slid down his neck, landing with the Light of Nedarra held two-handed, point forward.

The Kazar saw the sword tip, and with amazing agility and speed, he changed course in midair. But Khara wasn't about to be satisfied with merely causing the big cat to stumble. She anticipated his move and swung her sword so it was horizontal, blade-on toward the Kazar. He hit Khara's weapon with his left shoulder.

The fabled Light of Nedarra wasn't merely a symbol. It was as sharp as metallurgy and theurgy would allow, and it cut deeply into the Kazar's shoulder. He landed like a sack of flour, with none of a cat's grace.

But there was no time for Khara to press her advantage. Chimera was on his feet, rushing forward as if he meant to trample her. Victory stepped in front of him and took the force of the blow. Chimera was so big, and moving with such power, that Victory fell onto his side, whinnying in shock, just as the Light of Nedarra came down fast and hard, biting into the monster's arm.

The crowd gasped as Chimera's right arm fell to the ground. Blood sprayed like rain, and he bellowed in anguish. "I will eat your eyes while you still live!" he cried.

The Kazar was wounded. So was Chimera. But Khara was, too, though she concealed it miraculously well, drawing power from her sword and her own indomitable will. Still, I knew that much of the blood saturating her jerkin was her own. And I saw the way she clenched her jaw in pain with every move.

Chimera didn't take the loss of his arm well. He hissed and roared. He picked it up off the ground and tried to reattach it. "Your Chimera's as stupid as you are, Murdano," the Kazar taunted. But it was clear he was favoring his left side.

I sensed a change in mood of the two armies. No one had expected Khara to be able to seriously wound both her opponents. A shiver of hope shot through me, but I knew it was insane.

Tobble nudged me. I followed his gaze. Gambler was whispering instructions to the young, spotted felivet, who quickly melted back into the Kazar's army.

Behind the enraged, foot-stomping Chimera, the Kazar was up and rushing at Khara, but not gracefully. The cut on his shoulder made him awkward—awkward but still terrifyingly dangerous.

The Kazar charged and Khara dodged. He'd lost none of his killer instincts, but as he tried to take her down, he was forced to pivot on his wounded side. He skidded onto his back, momentarily helpless.

That moment was all Khara needed. The Light of

Nedarra blazed bright as she raised it, two-handed, and brought it down with all her failing power.

The sword bit deep. A red seam opened in the Kazar's chest and he rolled to his side, instantly dead.

The Kazar's personal guards surged forward, drawing their swords as they did. But before they could kill the girl who had killed their lord and master, they found their way blocked by two felivets, hackles raised, razor-sharp teeth bared.

"It's single combat," Naleese said calmly. "None of you were invited."

The leader of the guards swung his sword at Naleese. Gambler readied to pounce, but Naleese had already launched herself at the guard, digging her foreclaws into his sides and sinking her teeth into his throat.

The Kazar's guards weren't easily frightened, though. With Naleese occupied, they liked their chances against a single big cat.

They did not like their chances nearly as much when the spotted felivet leapt to join Gambler, accompanied by three more of his kind.

The guards were well trained, motivated, and experienced. But it takes a great deal of courage for a human to challenge a felivet. It takes stupidity or sheer madness to fight six felivets, and the guards were neither stupid nor mad. They receded grudgingly, dragging along what was left of the soldier who'd fought Naleese.

Gambler and his felivet crew chased the guards into the army behind them, following them as they stumbled and crawled beneath the terramants.

"The Kazar's done for! Finish the girl!" the Murdano shouted exultantly.

"Yes. Finish me," Khara said, facing the one-armed reptile.

Chimera took a step forward, as if he planned to charge, but it was a feint. Instead, he hurled his short spear. It flew with grim accuracy and hit Khara almost exactly where she'd already been wounded.

"Ah!" she cried, falling to her knees.

Chimera was on her in a flash, battering her with his remaining hand. Khara was so small beneath Chimera's great bulk, her strength sapped. I knew, with awful certainty, that she was about to die.

On her knees in the mud, one arm useless, a spear protruding from her shoulder and weighing her down, with her life's blood turning the ground crimson, Khara swung the Light of Nedarra one last time. I heard the sound of metal hitting bone.

She tried to stand, but it was too much for her. Khara looked at me and I saw her eyes, stricken.

"I'm . . . sorry," she said. She fell onto her back, legs

sprawled. Her eyes closed.

"No! Nooo!" Tobble cried, as Chimera loomed above her, and my heart withered inside of me.

"Don't die yet, girl. Don't die until I've ripped out your heart!" the monster screamed.

At the very edge of unconsciousness, if not death itself, Khara moved her sword just as Chimera prepared to tear her apart. All she could manage to do was raise it vertically and rest the hilt on the ground.

Chimera waved to the crowd, victorious and preening. Nodding to the Murdano, he began to kneel down next to Khara's limp body, his clawed hand prepared to do its worst. But he was distracted, and Khara was not.

It took him a moment to realized that he'd impaled himself on her sword.

His only word, his last word, was a surprised "You?" And then he toppled to the ground.

Khara lay helpless, her sword stuck deep into Chimera's writhing body.

The Murdano, clearly unsettled, finally seemed to dredge up a small nugget of courage. He pushed through the guards around him, drew his jewel-encrusted sword, and advanced on Khara.

I heard Renzo cry "Khara!" and spur his horse, but the crowd had closed in, and his route was blocked.

I looked for Gambler. He was lost somewhere amid the Dreylander army.

Neither Renzo nor Gambler would be quick enough.

There was no one to stop the Murdano from killing the Lady of Nedarra.

No one but a small dairne with a very small sword. And her loyal wobbyk companion.

39
The Final Battle

We leapt off Doona. Some part of my mind registered how ridiculous we must have looked, two little creatures facing enormous armies.

We stood in front of Khara, as if somehow we could protect her. She lay just behind us, drained and shattered.

The Murdano, the most powerful person in all of Nedarra, the man who had doomed so many dairnes, who had driven us to the very edge of extinction, grinned down at me.

"Must I kill you two first?" the Murdano asked.

"Yes." I managed a bare whisper. My mouth was bone-dry, my stomach twisted into knots.

"Well then . . ." He swung his sword in a sweeping backhand meant to cut me through the middle. I stumbled back, and by sheer luck the blow struck my shield.

Tobble charged, with insane wobbyk fury, at the Murdano, climbing up his chain mail until he'd reached the man's head. Clawing, biting, screeching, Tobble did his best, but the Murdano caught him on the tip of his sword and tossed him several feet. He landed hard and did not move.

"Tobble!" I screamed. I held out my sword, half hoping the Murdano would impale himself the way Chimera had. He sneered, and with an almost casual flick of his wrist, his sword knocked mine from my hand. It flew a few feet and landed in a puddle of mud.

There was not the slightest chance I could reach it.

"Byx." Khara's voice was a gasp of pain. I glanced over—it was all I could do, as I was busy preparing to die—and realized she was holding something toward me.

The Murdano raised his sword high, still grinning, ready to kill me and then Khara. Ready to kill thousands upon thousands.

The hilt!

Khara was holding the hilt of her sword toward me.

I took two quick steps back, keeping my eye on the Murdano, and there it was, practically jumping into my hand.

I had a bad grip on it—backward, more spear than knife—but it wasn't as heavy as I'd expected. Indeed, it felt not just light, but almost alive.

The Murdano began his downward swing. I threw myself forward to get inside of the deadly descending blade. As I did, I raised my right hand, the hand holding the Light of Nedarra.

The Murdano saw, too late. Too late to stop his swing or arrest his forward momentum. The blade's point was just inches from his heart as he windmilled like a man at the edge of a cliff.

But he couldn't stop. Not until two inches of the blade had sliced through his gold chain mail, his fine silk doublet, his undergarments, his flesh. His look of shock confirmed, as did the red blood flowing, that I had cut him.

But it wasn't yet fatal. He wouldn't die of the cut I'd inflicted. No. He'd die when I felt, coursing through me, all the pain and rage of finding my family slaughtered because of this evil man. He'd die when I looked into his wide, horrified eyes and cried, "For the dairnes!"

I grabbed the hilt firmly in both hands, and I plunged the Light of Nedarra through his heart.

40
A Time of Marvels

The troops of the Army of Peace, with General Varis in command, arrived the next day.

They were prepared for war.

Instead they found peace. A tentative peace. Fragile, uncertain, vulnerable.

But peace nevertheless.

The two opposing armies had agreed to withdraw, separated by a distance of five miles. Negotiations would be taking place at a simple campsite composed of a dozen tents circling a large bonfire.

A thin veil of snow was falling. Tobble and I were amusing ourselves watching flakes melt as they twirled toward the fire. It was late afternoon, and the first day of diplomacy had already concluded. Most of the negotiators were in their tents, and more would be joining us in the days to come.

"They're here!" I nudged Tobble, pointing. "I see General Varis and Bodick."

"Should we go meet them?"

I grinned. "It'd be the polite thing."

We sauntered toward the intimidating column of cavalry, spearmen, and archers. Of humans and raptidons, wobbyks and ragglers. Our plan was to act perfectly casual, as if nothing much had happened.

It was silly, especially given everything that had happened. But I suppose we were a bit giddy with relief.

We walked slowly, and Tobble leaned on my arm for support. He'd been badly bruised in yesterday's battle, and his left paw was swollen to twice its normal size.

"Good day to you, General Varis," I called.

"Good . . . g-good. . . good day?" he sputtered. "What do you mean, 'good day'? What is the news?"

"Well, we were just about to brew some tea," said Tobble. "Will you join us?"

"It's tannamint," I added. "Very refreshing."

"Will I . . . Did you say *tea*?" The general's face was ruddy with frustration. "Where *is* everyone?"

Bodick threw up her hands. "Quit playacting and tell us what's going on!"

"All right," Tobble said, relenting. "There's much to tell."

"My apologies," I said, adopting a more serious tone. "To begin with, the Lady was badly wounded. Renzo is with her, and she's being cared for by the chief doctors of both armies."

"And will she recover?" Varis asked.

"To be honest, we feared for her," I said. "She was injured with both arrow and sword. But just an hour ago, I had to soothe a Dreylander doctor who was fleeing her tent. She threatened to disembowel him if he gave her one more foul-tasting concoction to drink."

General Varis threw back his head and laughed. "That is heartening indeed," he said. He leaned forward in his saddle. "But what of the Kazar? And the Murdano?"

"Even though she was wounded, the Lady challenged them to single combat."

"More like two on one," Tobble said.

"She killed the Kazar," I said, still awed by her bravery. "Then she killed the Murdano's champion."

"By herself?" The general's mouth dropped open.

"Well," I said, "she had a very good sword."

"And the Murdano himself?" General Varis asked. "Is he our prisoner?"

"I'd be more than happy to take charge of jailer duties," Bodick offered.

"Alas," Tobble said, "the Murdano is also no longer with us."

Bodick's eyes went wide. "The Lady got him, too?"

"Not exactly," said Tobble. He turned to me and held out a paw.

General Varis and Bodick exchanged an incredulous look. "Impossible," said the general.

"No," Bodick said. "No."

"Yes," Tobble said. "The killer of the dairnes met a rather poetic fate."

I was not nearly as proud of myself as Tobble was. I would have to live with the indelible memory of leaning into the hilt of Khara's sword.

I would have to remember forever the way its blade had cut through skin and organ and sinew.

I would always have the image of the Murdano turning disbelieving eyes to me and mouthing just two words: "A dairne?"

As I'd watched his eyes grow dull, I'd recited the names of my family members, one by one. Was it revenge? I suppose. But was it also justice? Yes. I hoped so, anyway.

"I would rather have seen him imprisoned for his sins," I said. "But we . . . I . . . had no choice."

General Varis and Bodick nodded solemnly. They both knew how I felt. They understood the impossibly heavy burden that came with taking a life. Any life.

General Varis ordered the Army of Peace to withdraw five miles, in keeping with the other two armies. Once that had happened, he and Bodick joined us by the fire. "What now?" Bodick asked, warming her hands near the flames.

"Now," I said, "we talk. The Lady's ordered that representatives of the six governing species, along with an overlooked seventh species"—I nodded at Tobble—"come together here, to discuss and negotiate."

"Negotiate," General Varis repeated, sounding both hopeful and dubious.

"Rorid Headcrusher is coming to speak for the raptidons," I said. "The terramants believe they must have three of their own to speak for their people. You, General Varis, if you're willing, can speak for humans, along with the Lady. No less than Queen Pavionne herself will arrive to speak for natite interests. Naleese has agreed to speak for the felivets."

"Ah," said Bodick. "So that explains the canal we noticed some terramants digging."

"We asked them—politely, I assure you—to use their tunneling skills to dig a short channel to the river. It will expedite the arrival of the natites."

"I assume you, Tobble, will represent that seventh, overlooked species?" asked the general.

"I will," said Tobble proudly.

"And you, Byx, the dairnes?" Bodick asked.

"Sabito's confirmed that Maxyn will be coming tomorrow. He and I will speak for the dairnes together. By then, we hope the Lady will be well enough to be part of the discussion."

"Part of?" Varis echoed. "She's the one who destroyed both tyrants. She's the one who brought us peace. Let her speak her wishes, and we'll all shout yes."

"That's not what the Lady wants," I said. "She plans to obey the will of the assembled council. She'll serve. But not rule."

"Serve, but not rule?" Frowning, Bodick turned the phrase over, considering it.

"The Lady has the whole world at her feet," General Varis protested. "No one will oppose her."

"Yes," I agreed. "But the Lady is, for all of that, still my friend, Khara. Even with the world at her feet, she'll step aside."

"Very strange," Bodick said.

"Beyond strange," the general agreed. "Still, I've sworn to serve her. And if she wishes to serve, rather than rule . . ." He shrugged. "Very strange. But we live in a time of marvels. A war's been stopped and two terrible tyrants have been laid low, all by a girl, a dairne, and a wobbyk. Who knows what wonders are yet to come?"

41
The Declaration of the Seven

After eight days of talks, often heated, but more often quite tedious, the representatives issued a proclamation that became known as "The Declaration of the Seven."

Khara had persuaded the council to make wobbyks a governing species. It was not a difficult decision, given their amazing bravery in the face of daunting odds.

I knew every word of the declaration by heart.

On this day, after much strife and bloodshed, we, the council representing all governing species, do most solemnly vow that from this day until the end of all things, we shall nevermore make war upon one another.

The leaders of all lands will join to protect the lives and freedom of all species, to include (in alphabetical order) Dairnes,

Felivets, Humans, Natites, Raptidons, Terramants, and Wob-
byks, giving preference to none, but allowing each to find its
own path to happiness.

Dreyland, Nedarra, and the Seas beyond shall be governed by
rulers chosen by their people, and sworn to serve and protect
all species equally.

No subject of any species may ever again be deprived of life or
liberty without cause.

Dairnes agree to place members of their own species in every
realm, and the rulers of those realms agree to include Dairnes
in their councils, concealing nothing, so that lies and truth
may be plainly seen by all.

It was a simple document, only a page long, though everyone knew that the details would be hashed out for many more
weeks. A great deal of work was left to be done.

No one had ever before considered allowing the common
folk to choose their leaders. Until something called an "elec-
tion" could be held, Dreyland would be ruled temporarily by
Naleese and her consort, Gambler. Queen Pavionne would
continue to govern her portion of the seas—there was no question that she was loved by her people—and begin the work of
convincing other natite rulers to accept the Declaration.

The council also gave temporary rule of Nedarra to Khara. She, however, argued strenuously against the idea. "I'm flattered by the offer," she told them. "But I'm young. I have no experience."

They replied that she'd stopped a war, which was far more than most rulers managed to do.

Once she began to soften, ever so slightly, on the idea of leading, the representatives suggested that Khara should call herself "Queen of Nedarra." She simply laughed. "I'm no queen and I never will be," she said flatly. "Being called the Lady of Nedarra is more honor than I deserve. And certainly all the honor I can bear."

When Gambler learned the council had chosen him to rule Dreyland alongside Naleese, he reacted in typical Gambler style. "You want me to be surrounded by advisers and counselors, pestering me for answers to problems I can't even imagine? To eat food that I did not hunt for myself? To tell people what to do? I will not! Never!"

Naleese had given him a long look and said, in her hoarse feline whisper, "Gambler." And that had been that. Mighty Gambler—fearsome, dangerous, deadly Gambler of tooth and claw and rippling muscle—changed his tune after one word from Naleese. It reminded me of the secret looks and private murmurs that had passed between my mother and father not so long ago.

The thought of my dear parents brought back cold waves of sadness. I'd never had the time, amid all the madness of the past few months, to properly grieve for my family. I stayed with Khara and the others for days that soon became weeks, but all the while I knew what I must do.

One evening, I found Khara out walking at sunset, dressed in something rather like the poacher's clothing she'd worn when I'd first met her what seemed a lifetime ago. We dairnes can move very quietly—though nothing close to felivet quiet—when we choose to. Still, I didn't surprise her. Without bothering to turn, she said, "Good evening, Byx."

"Good evening, my lady."

"Oh, please don't call me that. Not you, Byx. I have to be just plain Khara to someone, or I'll lose my mind."

"All the praise and adoration annoys you?" I teased.

She shook her head ruefully. "At first I felt the need to correct people, to remind them that I'm still just a girl, and that I couldn't have done anything without my loyal friends, but . . ." She waved her hand in a gesture of resignation. "That got to be exhausting after a while, so now I just let it all roll off me. It's not healthy to have people adore you, Byx. It's why I'll never be queen. I can't bear all the bowed heads and worshipful expressions."

"Maybe you should speak with Queen Pavionne," I suggested. "She seems to be much the same sort of person as you."

With her left hand, Khara picked up a handful of snow. She squeezed it into a ball and tossed it far into the trees. The doctors weren't sure if she would ever regain total use of her right arm.

"I did talk to Pavionne," she said. "She's very wise."

"I had that same impression."

"You know what she told me? She said, 'Khara, quit complaining and correcting people. It's not really about you. People have been through a very bad time, and they need to believe that someone will be brave enough and strong enough to help them make life better.'"

"As you said, Queen Pavionne is wise."

Khara looked in my eyes and sighed. "You've come to tell me you're leaving."

"Maxyn can manage the task of truth telling."

"Yes. But who will manage the task of being my friend, Byx?"

"I'll always be your friend, Khara," I said. "But I have something, long delayed, that I must see to."

She nodded. "I understand."

"Actually, that's why I'm here. I want to ask your permission to travel to the last place that was my home."

"You'll never need my permission to do anything, Byx. But since you seem determined to give me the queenly powers I don't want, I will, in queenly style, give you a command."

"A command?"

She looked at her feet. "There is an, um, an event that I would like you to attend when you return from your trip."

I broke into a grin. "Would this event also involve Renzo?"

"Yes," she said, trying to sound nonchalant. "Renzo will also be involved in the, um, event."

"No power in the world could stop me attending the, um, event," I said. "When will the, um, event occur?"

"In three months."

"Then I will be there. I may even bring a gift. Or perhaps two gifts. One for your birthday, and one for the, um, event."

She laughed. "This is why I need you, Byx. I've grown so grand that no one else will mock me."

"Not even Renzo?"

"Good point." She smiled. "I can always count on him for that."

"Always."

"When do you leave?" Khara asked. Her voice was soft as the breeze.

"Tomorrow, at first light." It was my turn to sigh. "I dread telling Tobble that I'm going."

"You don't mean to take him with you?"

"No, Tobble has had enough adventures. He should be with his people." I wiped away a tear. "And that is what I intend to tell him."

Khara put her left arm around my shoulder, and we

watched the sun slip from view as darkness spread across the land.

"It's funny," she said.

"What?"

"When we met—"

"You mean when you captured me."

"I *mean*," Khara said, "when I saved your life."

I nodded. "That, too."

"When we met, you were the last creature on earth I dreamed I'd come to rely on. But you became the first one I turned to when wisdom was required. And the only one, in the end, who could save us."

My heart swelled at her words, though I knew they weren't true. "We're only here because of you, Khara."

"I'd beg to differ," she said.

"And I would gently, but respectfully, argue the point."

Khara laughed. "Spoken like a true ambassador."

"Well, I've had a bit of experience."

"We did the best we could, Byx," said Khara. "And that's all we ever need to know."

42
Travels with Tobble

At dawn, I saddled Achoo and prepared to leave.

The night before, I'd firmly explained to Tobble that I would be traveling solo. He was my dearest friend, I told him. But the task before me was a grim one, and I couldn't ask him to join me.

At which point Tobble explained to me, also very firmly, that I was going nowhere without him.

I knew better than to argue with a wobbyk.

We'd hoped to make a quiet departure without waking anyone, but we found Renzo by Achoo's side, double-checking the pony's readiness for travel.

"You didn't have to see us off," I told him.

He reached for our packs. "I wasn't about to let you sneak off without saying goodbye."

"You hate goodbyes," said Tobble.

"True." Renzo paused to adjust Achoo's bit.

"We'll see you soon enough," I said. "I hear that an event is in store."

"You'd better be there," said Renzo, grinning. "I may need moral support."

"What event?" Tobble demanded.

"It's a secret," I said.

"I hate secrets," Tobble grumbled. "Almost as much as goodbyes."

I mounted Achoo, and Renzo gave Tobble a boost. Standing back, hands on hips, Renzo shook his head.

"Stay out of trouble, you two," he said. "Unless I'm there for the fun."

We rode past the circle of tents and over a small hill. The morning was hushed, fresh with a frosting of snow. Our breaths made little clouds as we moved.

"It's so quiet," Tobble said.

And for a few minutes it was.

Until it wasn't.

We turned a sharp right, past a stand of dense trees, to a stunning sight.

The Army of Peace was arrayed in perfect order on both sides of the road. General Varis was there, and Bodick. Maxyn, Sabito, Gambler, and Naleese were waiting, too.

As we passed, each soldier came to attention. General Varis cried, "Three cheers for two great heroes!" and wild cries rang out.

Khara waited at the end of the line. A breathless Renzo was there as well. I sent him a questioning look and he winked. "I took a shortcut."

With her good arm, Khara drew the Light of Nedarra and held it aloft. I suspect she wiped away a tear, but since my own eyes were streaming, I couldn't be sure.

Half a league on, Tobble spoke for the first time. "Poor old General Varis, he made a mistake. I hope he's not embarrassed."

"Mistake?"

"Yes, he meant to say 'three cheers for our hero,' but he said '*two* great heroes.'"

I turned around and gave Tobble a playful shove. "Sometimes, Tobble, you are a bit slow to grasp the obvious."

Our journey took weeks, uneventful travel tracing many of the same roads and paths we'd once followed while in peril. Khara had ensured that we had jewels and gold coins for our journey, so we bought food from farmers along the way, and some nights we even stopped at inns. Frequently we were offered beds in the homes of perfect strangers, who, much to my embarrassment, knew us by reputation.

I had become "the Truth Teller," with capital letters, as

though it were my official title. And Tobble was known far and wide as "the Prince of Wobbyks."

As we rode away from one particularly enthusiastic village, Tobble said, "I wish people wouldn't call me Prince of Wobbyks. I really don't enjoy that at all."

"Tobble?"

"Yes?"

"Tobble, what species am I?"

"You're a dairne, of course."

"Yes. And what special ability do dairnes possess?"

A long pause followed. "I would like to withdraw my earlier remark."

"Yes, I thought you might."

The farther we got from the capital and the battlefields, the less people knew about everything that had happened in the north. The land was less populated, with fewer farms and more forests and meadows. The climate was warmer, too. The trees still had leaves and flowers still bloomed, filling the air with the sweet scents of jasmine and moonflower.

One afternoon, we rode through the Forest of Null, eating what we had in our saddlebags, along with berries we'd picked along the way.

"This is all seeming more familiar," I said. It was a melancholy feeling. I'd been raised in this part of Nedarra, but we'd had to stay on the move constantly. No one place had ever truly been home. Home was simply wherever my family happened to be.

On a section of the trail hemmed by thick undergrowth, I caught the scent of something disturbing on the wind.

"Do you smell that, Tobble?" I asked.

He sniffed the air. "Yes. And I hear movement in the woods to either side."

A man stepped into our path. He was stocky, dressed in green garments meant to mimic the color of the trees. He had a long sword in his hand and was resting it casually on his shoulder. "Halt!" he cried.

More men rushed onto the pathway behind us.

"Poachers!" Tobble whispered.

"Yes. The same band that Khara once traveled with."

"The same band that very nearly killed you, Byx."

I reined in Achoo, who, true to his name, sneezed enthusiastically. "What is it you wish?" I asked the first man, feeling surprisingly calm.

He laughed. "Dairne pelt and wobbyk stew, of course."

I turned to Tobble. "I believe this poacher means to harm us. Do you suppose he remembers the young, dark-haired lad who used to scout for him?"

"What about him?" the man asked suspiciously.

"Well, first, he was no lad, but rather a young woman."

"So he was a she. So what?"

"So she is now a lady. In fact, *the* Lady, ruler of all Nedarra. We're her friends, and I should probably tell you that if any harm came to us, she'd be here in an instant, with an army of soldiers who worship her and love us."

The poacher licked his lips nervously. A voice from behind yelled, "They lie!"

"She's a dairne," came another voice, this one tremulous. "They aren't able to lie."

It wasn't strictly true, but I didn't see any need to correct him.

"And if that's not enough to make you step aside . . ." I drew my short sword. "I must mention that although I despise violence and wish only peace, I have taken a life."

The poacher laughed, but uncertainly. He was a trapper, not someone interested in the business of sword fighting. "Whose life did you take?"

"The life of the Murdano of Nedarra."

The poacher blinked. Of all the things I might have said, he surely didn't expect that answer.

"I'm not proud of it," I added. "And I hope never to take another life. But if you don't stand aside . . ."

I let my words hang in the air. After a minute, during which the poacher tried his best to look bold and threatening, he stepped away.

I sheathed my sword. "There's peace in the land," I said, softening my voice. "The harsh rule of the Murdano led many men to earn a living by robbing or poaching. But the Lady is not the Murdano. A man willing to do work will find it. A man willing to live under the law will see that the law is his shield. Go to the Lady and make your peace with her. She's merciful."

To my surprise, the man took off his hat as a sign of respect and said, "Peace? That word has a good sound to it."

"Tell the Lady that Byx has sent you. She may find a use for you and your men."

When we were well away, Tobble said, "That might have been a good time to mention you're the Truth Teller and I'm the Prince of Wobbyks."

"You know that's just a title of honor, right? It doesn't grant you any power."

"Power? Pff. I have no desire for power. Or wealth. Or fame."

"Tobble."

"All right. Once again, I'd like to withdraw my earlier remark." He sighed. "It's no fun traveling with a dairne."

When we came at last to a particular oak, broad-limbed and welcoming, I reined in.

"Why are we stopping?" Tobble asked.

"Because I remember that tree. I know where we are."

"Ah."

"This next part I wish to travel alone," I said, and for once Tobble did not argue.

43
Returning

I cannot, will not, tell the full story of my next few hours. I'll only say that I found what I knew I must: the sun-bleached bones of everyone I'd once loved.

Even knowing what I would find, I was unprepared for the knife of pain that cut through me. I half fell, half dismounted, from my pony.

Kneeling on the ground, I gave in to the grief I'd held at bay for so long. I howled like an animal. I beat my fists against my chest. I wept.

I don't know how long it went on. Time disappears, I suppose, when you need it to.

At last I stood, squeezed the last of my tears from my burning eyes, and wiped my face. I found Achoo munching grass not far away, and unpacked the shovel I'd brought for just this purpose.

I began to dig.

It was hard labor, but I took grim satisfaction in it. It distracted me from the dread of what I had to do next.

I dug a single hole. I made it less than my own height, so that I could climb out without too much difficulty. When I surfaced, dirty and sweaty and sore, I saw that each small pile of bones had been decorated with a tiny red flower.

"This part you must not do alone," said Tobble.

"I'm the only one left of my pack, Tobble. The only one."

"The last of your pack," he said softly. "But not the last of your kind."

With great care, we gathered the bones, and as we worked I turned my mind to memories of better times.

I saw my mother's sweet smile. I heard my father's wise proverbs. I recalled my siblings, rowdy and teasing, gentle and loving. I remembered Myxo, our valiant pathfinder, and Dalyntor, our teacher and the keeper of our history.

Who would keep that history alive now?

Tobble found a small sapling and replanted it at the grave as a marker. We spent the night in the woods, a few dozen yards away.

In the morning I said, "Thank you, Tobble. Thank you, best of all possible friends."

He nodded. "Of course. You would do the same for me, Byx. So where do we go now?"

"Oh, we head back north, Tobble. There's to be an event."

"Ah, yes. The *secret* event." He wagged a finger at me. "There's a reason I haven't hounded you about that. I suspect I already know what it is."

"Does it involve two humans that we both love?"

"It does indeed!" Tobble cried.

We mounted up, and I paused to take one last look back at the gravesite. I hoped the sapling would take root and grow. But I wasn't sure I would ever return to find out.

"Byx?" Tobble asked.

"Yes?"

"After the . . . event, what will you do? Will you go find other dairnes and live with them?"

"I don't know, Tobble. Will you return to Bossyp? To be with other wobbyks?"

"I always thought I would." Tobble shrugged. "But it doesn't seem quite as important anymore. You know?"

"I do," I said softly. "I do know."

We rode away in silence. We hadn't gone far when I scented something off to one side of the path. I knew that smell. Or at least my heart knew it, even if my head didn't. It had the strange familiarity of a dream fragment. Spurred on by instinct and distant memory, I rode deep into the forest.

And there it was. Phantom Mere, just as I remembered it.

The sandy shore. The criller trees, with their shiny, light gold leaves. The dark surface, like polished stone. Even the blue squirrels were there, chittering in annoyance at our intrusion.

"See that vine?" I said to Tobble. "My siblings and I used to swing out from it, then land in the lake." I gave a small laugh. "Well, *they* did, anyway. I was too afraid."

"You? Afraid?"

"Always and forever," I said. "I'm beginning to think that's how life works."

"Are we stopping here?" Tobble asked. "The horses are well watered."

"Yes, but I'm not. Do you know what I need, Tobble? I need a swim."

I checked the icy water with a long stick to be sure it was as deep as I recalled. Two silver fish darted past.

As I clambered to a low-hanging branch, I felt a familiar shiver of anticipation and dread, and for a moment, I was the old Byx, with all her hopes and fears and longings.

Then I kicked off as hard as I could, swung far out over the pond, and let go.

EPILOGUE

EPILOGUE
Ten Years Later . . .

"All we have left to do is hang the official portrait of the high governor and we'll be done," I said, brushing dust from my fur as I looked around with a critical eye.

I gazed out the window at the bustling Isle of Scholars and the calm harbor beyond. I'd been working at the Academy for years, restoring the dairne level of the Pillar of Truth, but I never tired of the view.

The Pillar included floors devoted to the study of both dairnes and wobbyks. When dairnes had been presumed extinct, this floor had been used for storage. Now it was filled with leather-bound books, maps, drawings, and transcriptions of oral histories.

My two young dairne assistants, a boy and a slightly older girl, raced to lift the portrait, draped in velvet. The hook was already waiting in the wall, along with a tall ladder nearby. They maneuvered precariously but managed to get the painting attached.

"Shall I uncover it, Mistress Byx?" asked Laryx, the girl.

"Yes, please do." I'd already seen the portrait, but the children had not.

She pulled away the drape, revealing the familiar face, older by ten years. People whispered that Khara never seemed to age, but I saw the signs. The cares of her office had added a few faint lines, along with a certain wisdom and gravity. It was the face of a woman of accomplishment: Kharassande the Great, High Governor of Nedarra, ruling by the choice of a free and united people.

Kharassande the Great to many.

Khara, dear old friend, to me.

Into the room burst two small demons in the form of human children, a boy and a girl. The twins were five years old, with the dark, wavy hair of their mother and the mischievous smile of their father.

"Auntie Byx, do you still have any of that butterbee cake?" asked Alessa.

"I do, if my assistants have left some," I said, pointing them to a table. They fell upon the cake like wild beasts—or five-year-old humans, which I'd learned was much the same thing. I'd recently been visited by Gambler and Naleese and their four children, and by comparison, the young felivets had been models of perfect behavior.

Renzo appeared at the doorway. "Hello there, Byx," he said. "Or do I have to call you Byx the Gharri now?"

I laughed. I'd only last month been honored with the title of "Gharri," and I still had a hard time believing it. The label was reserved for the most influential and respected scholars at the Academy.

"Of course, I'm the only dairne Gharri," I told Renzo. "There aren't that many of us. Yet, anyway."

Khara entered. "Are our horrible children bothering you?" she asked as she embraced me.

"Oh, they're monsters where cake is involved, but we'll survive."

Renzo gazed up at the portrait of his wife. "Pity you don't look that beautiful in real life, Khara."

She smacked his shoulder playfully and they linked arms, as in love as they'd ever been.

Alessa dashed in from an anteroom. "We found Tobble!"

"He was snoring!" Carlo exclaimed.

"Snoring?" came an outraged, and very sleepy, reply. "Why, I was studying an ancient scroll about wobbyks. I closed my eyes to think more clearly!"

Tobble shuffled out, rubbing sleep from his eyes. Seeing Khara, he bowed low. It was the polite thing to do when encountering a leader, and he was nothing if not polite.

"I was contemplating the nature of the universe," Tobble grumbled, "when I was beset by these young hooligans!"

Tobble hadn't yet had children with Nerble, the wonderfully patient wobbyk he'd married just a year earlier. Despite his complaints, he doted on the twins.

Khara cocked her head at the newly hung portrait. "Do I look a bit grumpy?"

Renzo drew her close. "Not in the least. You look lovely. And I will offer to fight anyone who says different. Unless, you know, he's bigger than I am."

"I wonder, Byx," said Khara, "amid all the comfort and ease you have now, do you ever miss the days when we were racing from here to there, in constant danger, running for our lives?"

"No," I said. "Not at all."

Tobble shook his head. "I sure don't."

"Me neither," Renzo agreed.

"Nor do I," said Khara.

It didn't take a dairne to know that all four of us had lied.

Acknowledgments

Endless thanks to my amazing editor, Tara Weikum, as well as Jenn Corcoran, Audrey Diestellkamp, Vaishali Nayak, Emily Zhu, Renée Cafiero, Sarah Homer, Barb Fitzsimmons, Alison Donalty, Jenna Stempel-Lobell, Chris Kwon, Patty Rosati, Andrea Pappenheimer, Suzanne Murphy, and all the other folks at HarperCollins who've helped bring *Endling* to life; and to my wonderful agent, Elena Giovanazzo, at Pippin Properties, Inc.

DON'T MISS THIS SNEAK PEEK
at Katherine Applegate's bestselling
book *The One and Only Bob*, sequel to
the Newbery Award winner *The One and Only Ivan*!

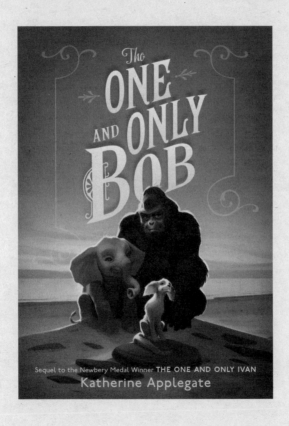

confession

Look, nobody's ever accused me of being a good dog.

I bark at empty air. I eat cat litter. I roll in garbage to enhance my aroma.

I harass innocent squirrels. I hog the couch. I lick myself in the presence of company.

I'm no saint, okay?

and while i'm at it . . .

I may or may not have eaten a pepperoni pizza with anchovies when nobody was looking.

Also, I may or may not have eaten a coconut vanilla birthday cake when nobody was looking.

Also, I may or may not have eaten a Thanksgiving turkey (except for the stuffing—*way* too much rosemary) when nobody was looking.

Nobody looking. That seems to be the common thread.

As they say on the crime shows: motive and opportunity.

robert

Name's Bob.

I'm a mutt of uncertain heritage. Definitely some Chihuahua, with a smidgen of papillon on my father's side.

You're probably thinking I'm some wimpy lap dog. The kind you see poking out of an old lady's purse like a hairy key chain. But size ain't everything.

It's swagger. Attitude. You gotta have the moves.

Probably I shoulda been named Bruiser or Bamm-Bamm or Bandit, but Bob's what I got and Bob'll do me just fine.

Julia named me. Long time ago. She's my girl. She calls me "Robert" when I get on her nerves.

Happens pretty often, to be honest.

numero uno

There's an old saying about us dogs, goes like this: *It's no coincidence that man's best friend can't talk.*

Lemme tell you something. If we *could* talk to people, they'd get an earful.

You ever hear anyone mention man being dog's best friend?

Nope?

Didn't think so.

Way I've always figured it, end of the day, you gotta be your own best friend. Look out for numero uno.

Learned that one the hard way.

That's not to say I don't have a best pal. I do.

Gorilla, name of Ivan. Big guy and I go way, way back.

Gorilla and dog. Yep, I know. You don't see that every day. Long story.

I love that big ol' ape. Ditto our little elephant friend, Ruby.

They're the best.

The first time I met Ivan, I was a homeless puppy. Desperate, starving, all alone.

It was the middle of the night, and I'd slipped into the mall where Ivan lived in a cage. I wandered a bit, grateful for the warmth, confused by the weird assortment of sleeping animals I found there, checking every trash can for anything edible.

There was a small hole in a corner of Ivan's enclosure. He was fast asleep, cuddled up with a worn stuffed animal that looked like a weary gorilla.

He was snoring, and man, that guy snored like a pro.

In his open palm was a chunk of banana, and—I still get shivers when I think about this—I ate it right out of his hand.

Guy coulda squeezed his fingers shut and I woulda popped like a puppy balloon. But he just kept on sleeping.

And then—more shivers—I am either a maniac or the bravest dog on the planet, probably a little of both—I hopped up onto that big, round, furry tummy of his.

That's right. I climbed Mount Ivan.

Crazy, I know. I have no idea what I was thinking. Maybe I was so exhausted I went a little bonkers. Maybe he just looked so warm and cozy that I figured it was worth taking a chance.

I did my bed boogie. Dogs don't feel right till we do a quick dance before settling.

Once I had things just so, I lay down in a little puppy lump and rode the waves on that tummy like a puny boat on a great brown sea.

When Ivan opened his eyes the next morning, he didn't seem surprised in the least to find a puppy snoozing on his belly. He refused to move until I woke up.

I think he was as glad as I was to have found a new friend.

the amazing history of
man's best friend

Before long, me and Ivan were best buddies.

We're an unlikely pair, sure. Ivan's calm and serene, a philosopher, an artist. I wish I could be more like that. No one's ever accused me of being levelheaded.

Hotheaded, sure.

And I can't talk pretty like Ivan can. I'm a street dog, after all. And proud of it.

Still, we clicked, in a way I never had with humans. "Man's best friend"? No way. "Gorilla's best friend"? You bet.

Seems to me the first time I ever heard that phrase— "man's best friend"—was while I was watching TV with Ivan.

Back in the day, Ivan had this little television, and we watched a lot of stuff together. Old movies, Westerns, cartoons, you name it. Poor guy was stuck in a cage, didn't have a lot else to do except throw me-balls at gaping humans.

Anyways. Me and Ivan, big fans of the tube. Cat food commercials. Pro bowling. *Dancing with the Stars.* What's not to like?

Once we watched this special on the nature channel. It was called *The Amazing History of Man's Best Friend.* Show was all about famous dogs. There were rescue dogs and therapy dogs and war dogs and fire dogs and movie dogs and this dogs and that dogs. And between you and me, most of 'em were just plain overachievers.

Then they got to this dog named Hach-something-or-other. Hatchet-toe, maybe? Seems his owner died (for the record, I object to the word "owner," but we'll set that aside for now), and Hach-something-or-other sat around for over nine years in the same spot at the same train station, day after day, waiting for him to return.